Michael Hardcastle
in Yorkshire. After
in the Royal Army Educational Corps before
embarking on a career in journalism, working in a number of roles for provincial daily
newspapers from reporter to chief feature
writer.

He has written more than one hundred
children's books since his first was published
in 1966, but still finds time to visit schools
and colleges all over Britain to talk about
books and writing. In 1988 he was awarded
an MBE in recognition of his services to
children's books. He is married and lives in
Beverley, Yorkshire.

by the same author

The Fastest Bowler in the World

One Kick

Own Goal

Quake

Second Chance

Please Come Home

in the Goal Kings series

BOOK TWO: Eye for a Goal

Shoot-Out

Michael Hardcastle

Goal Kings
BOOK ONE

faber and faber
LONDON · BOSTON

First published in 1998
by Faber and Faber Limited
3 Queen Square London WC1N 3AU

Typeset by Avon Dataset, Bidford-on-Avon, Warwickshire
Printed and bound in England by Mackays of Chatham PLC,
Chatham, Kent

© Michael Hardcastle, 1998

Michael Hardcastle is hereby identified as author of this work in
accordance with Section 77 of the Copyright, Designs and
Patents Act 1988

A CIP record for this book
is available from the British Library

ISBN 0–571–19142–8

2 4 6 8 10 9 7 5 3 1

Contents

1 In and then Out

In the village of Rodale Kings, everyone was sure the junior football team was going to win something this season. Well, not quite everyone. Alex Todd didn't believe it. And Alex was the team's main striker.

He was sitting on the bench, having just been substituted in the closing stages of the game against Heathcroft Hawks. When he wasn't muttering he was shaking his head fiercely so that his dark hair, which fell in waves from a central parting, bounced angrily just above his eyes.

'How can you do this to me? How can you take me off when I was going to get my hat-trick?' he demanded. 'I mean, those were two *great* goals, *great*. I was bound to get another, bound to. Those Hawk defenders out there are scared to death of me. You saw what they were like, Sam.'

'Calm it, Alex, just calm it, son,' Sam Saxton ordered, putting his left arm round the boy's shoulders. 'They've got the measure of you. That's why you weren't getting anywhere, that's why you were beginning to annoy the ref. When, that is, you weren't sulking.'

Alex jumped to his feet, away from the coach's kindly touch. Kindness wasn't what he wanted. All he could think about was his reputation and his ambitions. 'I wasn't sulking!' he exploded. 'I don't sulk. I was just – well, *mad* with Lloyd. He gave me the pass all wrong, must've seen that big centre-back was pulling my shirt so hard it came out of my shorts. I told the ref but he must be blind because –'

He stopped only because he knew the coach was no longer listening to him. Sam Saxton was on his feet, yelling at one of his players. 'Marc, go for it! Go for it, son. Don't hang back.' Then, 'Oh yes, nice touch, Lloyd. Nice flick-on, son.'

In spite of the praise, and the cleverness of the exchanges between the midfielders, Rodale Kings didn't add to their tally against the Hawks. Marc Thrale's attempt at a lob from just inside the box was woefully wide of the target. Both teams as well as the scatterings of spectators heard his shriek of despair.

'I'd've put that away easily, no danger,' Alex pointed out, his anger not having prevented him from watching every detail of the play. His right hand kept brushing his surprisingly dense eyebrows as if he were trying to uproot them. It was a gesture that warned all who knew him that his agitation was building up quickly again.

'No doubt you would,' Sam agreed calmly. '*If* you'd been in the right frame of mind to take your time and achieve the necessary accuracy. You've been told a thousand times, Alex: I'm usually pleased with your skills. When, that is, you want to turn them on. What bothers me is your attitude. You've got to do something about that or –'

'There's nothing wrong with my attitude,' Alex shot back. 'I want to win, just like you. But I need to be out on the pitch, getting the goals. That's what I'm best at. If you –'

'Stop it, Alex! Just shut up for once,' Mr Saxton said heavily. 'You've been subbed and I gave you the reason. I didn't have to do that but I want to be fair. Well, now you've had your say and I've listened to it. But I don't want to hear any more. I've an entire team to think about. I'm no longer focusing on one rebellious individual. Got that?'

There was no reply. Alex had already moved away down the touchline, although the words had clearly reached him. He wanted to go to the dressing-room and grab the first shower before everyone else shared the hot water. But that wasn't allowed: anyone subbed had to sit out the rest of the match alongside the coach. The only way to get an early shower was to be sent off: but for that offence the minimum punishment would be to miss the next match for the Kings. And, depending on the gravity of the crime, it could be a great deal worse than that. Sam Saxton liked to demonstrate that he was a hard man when it came down to matters of discipline ('or *in*discipline, as I regard it,' he would emphasize every time the subject came up).

To Alex's irritation, nobody seemed to be taking the slightest bit of notice of him as he wandered about even though they must all

4

know who he was. After all, he'd scored the Kings' first two goals, the first admittedly a tap-in after good work on the deadball line by Marc but the second a real screamer from just inside the box. What's more, Alex had hit it with his left, and usually weaker, foot. The pace of the shot had surprised even him for the Hawks' goalkeeper had simply been left helpless as the ball rocketed past him into the top of the net. That, Alex recognized, had been the start of his troubles because the Hawks realized how good he was; thus he'd been subjected to what he believed was some illegal man-to-man marking and with his shirt being grabbed and his arm held and once a sharp jab in the pit of the stomach that the ref really ought to have spotted and punished. But, as he glanced round now, no one was giving him an appreciative smile or a murmured word of praise. All the attention was being concentrated on the pitch as the purple-and-white-shirted Kings pressed for the fourth goal that would boost their chance of moving up the League table.

'Go on, Lloyd, go on – have a go, have a go!' the coach was yelling now as the gangly midfielder deftly cut inside the tiring Heath-croft defence. Then, as he turned again, he stumbled and lost possession. But within moments he'd recovered his balance, fought for the ball again and then followed the shouted instructions by trying a shot. But his aim was poorer than his intentions and this time the goalie didn't even bother to move as the ball sailed away in the direction of the corner flag.

Lloyd despairingly ran his fingers through his abundant black hair and shrugged as he spun back towards midfield to await another chance following the goal-kick. His agony barely lasted as long as that for when Alex glanced at him the smile, the customary beam of happiness, was back on Lloyd's face. How could *anyone* raise a grin, let alone a smile, after missing a clear-cut goal attempt? Alex wondered. Lloyd ought to be mad at his failure and make himself do better next time.

Then, as he edged still nearer to the dressing-room, Alex saw Mrs Colmer, Lloyd's mother, wearing one of her typically colourful skirts (greens and reds and orange this time) in spite of the fact that it was a rather chilly and drab autumnal day. She, too, was smiling and seemed pleased with her son's achievements.

'Oh, hi, Alex,' she greeted him. 'You did well. Have to say, I'm surprised the coach decided to take you off when you showed such good form.'

'Thanks,' said Alex, thoroughly pleased that someone was taking the trouble to show sympathy for his misfortune. 'But Sam's the boss. Have to do what he says.'

'Oh, don't we just know it, don't we just,' Mrs Colmer agreed. But her smile didn't waver. If anything, it seemed brighter.

So Alex couldn't be sure whether Lloyd's mother really did have strong opinions about the man who coached, promoted and controlled Rodale Kings in the Highlea Sunday League. On the other hand, if she didn't she'd probably be the only parent, maybe even the only villager, who didn't have a view of Sam Saxton and his role with the team. In such a small community as their village, everyone usually had an opinion about everything that went on within its boundaries.

For instance, Alex knew exactly where his

father stood on the matter of the way the junior football team was run. Ricky Todd had expressed his views often enough, at home, on the touchline, and at club meetings.

Alex wished his father were here now instead of playing in a golf game that, he'd insisted, he simply couldn't get out of because his partner was an important customer so he had to look after him. 'But in between *my* shots to the green I'll be thinking of your shots on target, Alex, so don't let me down,' he'd promised. 'Make sure you score a couple for me. Oh, and stay out of trouble, OK? Don't let anybody mess you about for any reason at any time. Just remember this, too: you're *bound* to be the best player on the pitch today.'

Well, Alex doubted that Sam Saxton thought he'd been the best player against Heathcroft in spite of the two goals he'd scored (which, of course, were for himself as well as for his dad). After all, the coach had taken him off, allegedly for sulking. That, Alex could convince himself without difficulty, was rubbish. No other coach would remove a player who was about to snatch a hat-trick; *any* other coach would have been cheering him on, eager to see him add perhaps another double strike because of the form he was in. For the umpteenth time Alex wished his dad would take over the team. He'd transform the Kings, no doubt about that; he'd encourage them to play a different kind of attacking football, the kind that would suit Alex perfectly. And Alex, naturally, would keep his place permanently; he wouldn't have to worry that he might be dropped for some daft reason.

He worried about that now as he moodily watched the closing moments of the game. The Hawks seemed to have lost any bite they had and so it was the Kings who were still attacking with Alex's replacement, Dominic Allenby, providing some neat touches and then a shot that crashed against the crossbar. Just a few centimetres lower and the ball would have been in the net. So Dominic would have remained in Sam's mind for the next match against Clocklane the following Sunday.

Alex shivered. It was getting distinctly cold these days and he always hated to put on a track suit top; he liked to display his shirt with the magic 'nine' so that everyone could see he was the chief striker. The shorts were fairly short, too, though not as short as Josh Rowley's, and so he carried out a few vigorous exercises on the spot to bring some warmth back into his legs.

With the very last kick of the game Dominic drove another shot against the base of a post and then turned away in dismay as the final whistle prevented him from having the chance of knocking in the rebound. Alex joined in the applause that rang out from spectators as the players trooped from the pitch. He knew it would have looked good if he'd gone over to Dominic to sympathize over his near misses but he simply couldn't bring himself to do so. Dominic could so easily be picked in his place for the Clocklane game. If that happened then Alex was absolutely certain that Rodale Kings would not win anything this season. Nobody on this earth would be able to make up for the goals that Alex would've scored if he'd been in the side for every game.

'Did you a favour, you know, whatever you

think,' a voice suddenly broke in on Alex's thoughts just as the players piled into the dressing-room. 'That ref would have been sure to book you if you'd antagonized him once more. You know my rule, Alex: players stupid enough to get a booking don't play in the next match, however much I need 'em. Discipline is a very important element in the game, as I'm always telling you.'

'Oh, so I'll be in the team against Clocklane, then, Sam?' Alex, spirits suddenly rising, asked.

'Oh, I'm not promising that, son, not promising *anything* yet. You'll just have to wait and see.'

Before going into the kitchen, Dominic opened the cupboard under the stairs and slung his sports bag as far as it would go. It hit the far wall with a satisfying thwunk and then he softly closed the door again.

'So, how did it go today?' asked his dad as Dominic raided the fridge for a can of his favourite sugary fruit drink.

'Bad, bad, bad. Didn't get on until near the end and then I missed two goals; hit the crossbar once and the bottom of the post. Last kick of the game, that was. But the Kings won, of course.'

'Well, I'm pleased to hear something went right,' grinned Mr Allenby, who had his hands in a pudding bowl where he was rubbing butter into a mixture of flour and sugar. 'Feeling hungry?'

'Yeah, sort of.' In fact, Dominic thought he could eat non-stop for the rest of the day but he wasn't going to admit that. Although he appreciated all the trouble his dad went to in making tasty meals he believed he shouldn't risk a lack of fitness by eating too much of anything that could put weight on his already stocky frame.

'Well, thanks for the enthusiasm! I go to all this trouble just to feed you up and –'

'Oh, come on, Dad, you *love* cooking, you know you do. You tell people it's your way of relaxing after a hard day's driving. So . . .'

His father nodded. 'OK, I admit all that. But there is still the other purpose of keeping you healthy. And since you're definitely not going to be a jockey now I can feed you up, make sure you keep growing.'

Dominic rolled his eyes upwards at yet another reference to the old idea that he might become a jockey. Apparently, as a young child (anyway, at a time Dominic himself couldn't remember) he'd been unusually small, quite puny really, and his parents had feared he'd remain under-sized. So his dad, who liked almost everything to do with horse-racing, had taken comfort from the thought that in later life his only son could ride horses for a living and provide his parents with winning tips to make them rich. Nowadays, Dominic suspected his dad still regretted the fact he'd grown to a perfectly normal size.

Ken Allenby rubbed his hands dry, poured the mixture over some fruit in a fireproof bowl and checked on the oven before sliding it on to the middle shelf. 'So,' he smiled, 'you can manage some lamb cutlets followed by plum crumble, can you?'

'Oh, sure, Dad, thanks,' Dominic replied casually, turning his attention to a football magazine that he had left under the bread tin. He knew his father was looking him over critically and he didn't want any more talk about weight or future career prospects. But he hadn't quite managed to read his dad's mind after all.

'I suppose you could turn to boxing if you *did* fill out a bit more,' he remarked. 'Boxing is made of money, top boxers can make more than a lottery winner in one night. I mean, just think of being World Heavyweight Champion, Champion of the World, in the blue corner –'

'Dad, Dad, pack it in!' Dominic blazed. 'You know I'm not interested in any sport except football. So why do you go on about it?'

'You know, red hair's supposed to be a sign of aggression – you must know that,' Mr Allenby went on as if his son hadn't spoken. 'When I was your age my hair was a lot redder than yours is now, though you'd never guess it nowadays when I've hardly any left of any colour to speak of. But it's true, I could be a bit of a fists-up when somebody crossed me, like your Uncle Jimmy. Could be worth thinking about, Dom, if things don't go your way on the footie field.'

Dominic forced himself not to respond. His dad had a habit of chuntering on and on about almost anything at all when he was in the mood, the result, Dominic supposed, of spending so much time on his own at the wheel of his delivery van with no one to talk to apart from the occasional customer who had time for a chat. Then he spotted an item in the magazine about the unhappy fate of a Spurs player who'd been dropped and wasn't able to get his place back for almost a season because his replacement had performed brilliantly. If only he himself had scored today against the Hawks *he* might have taken Alex's place in the team for the next match.

As it was, he imagined the best he could hope for would be to be picked as one of the subs again. Whatever he did these days, he couldn't seem to persuade Sam Saxton to put him into the team from the kick-off.

'Come on, Dom, cheer up. You look as if you've lost a fiver and found a two pence piece. Things can't be as bad as all that!' his dad broke in on his thoughts again. 'Not still thinking about your old Kings, are you? I mean, you said they'd won, so what's the problem?'

Dominic knew there was no point in discussing his real feelings about football with someone who cared so little about the game but he had to say something. 'I'm thinking of packing it in – no, no, not football altogether, I'd never do that. Just the Kings, that's all. Find another team, one that'll play me all the time, not mess me about like Sam does. That's what I'm thinking about, thinking about all the time, if you must know.'

Suddenly, hunger overwhelmed him. The aroma of the cooking and the sight of a plate of lamb cutlets, heaped mashed potatoes and gravy was irresistible. So when his dad said 'Let's eat!' Dominic didn't delay a moment. For some minutes they ate in silence, both relishing the food. There was no doubt about it, his dad really knew how to cook a tasty meal. Which was just as well because his mum conceded she was pretty hopeless in the kitchen. On the other hand, everybody said that Jane Allenby was brilliant at her job as a midwife.

'So where would you look for a new team?' Mr Allenby asked with a note of unexpected sympathy in his voice. 'I mean, you've got to remember that your mum and I couldn't guarantee to take you to matches on a regular basis. We've both got jobs that take us away at all sorts of odd times. Surely one of the best things about the Kings is that their pitch is just down the road from us. You could even get there on your hands and knees if you had to! That's the beauty of living in a fairly small village. Everything is close to hand.'

'Yeah, I do realize that,' Dominic nodded, 'but if I can find the right team I'll also find a way of getting to their matches. I mean, *somebody* will help out if I need them. The main thing is, Dad, for me to play regular first team football. That's the only way I'll get anywhere, get to the top. It's the worst thing in the world to have to hang around as a sub and only get on to the pitch in the last few minutes, like today. Even if I'd scored everybody would still think I was only a reserve, not a first team player. Makes me feel second-rate and I'm going to prove I'm *first-rate*.'

'Good for you,' Mr Allenby murmured because there wasn't much else he could say. 'Now, get stuck into this plum crumble. I just have a tiny feeling this could be first-rate, so you deserve it.'

*

'Lunch won't be more than five minutes but you're home a bit earlier than usual,' Marina Saxton told her husband with a welcoming smile. 'Didn't any of the parents collar you for a private word? Or was the game so bad everyone needed to escape as fast as possible?'

Sam shook his head. 'No, it was a fair result. We won four-nil and that was about right, though I suppose we ought to have scored a couple more. But not many parents turned up. Don't know why. I mean, it's not a bad day for this time of year, is it?'

He prowled round the sitting-room in his customary restless manner after a match and his wife watched him as she checked saucepans and set out cutlery. Usually he complained that he was ravenous about this time on a Sunday but for once he hadn't even enquired what they'd be eating, which was a pity because she'd've been delighted to tell him it was his favourite pasta carbonara followed by banana-and-raisin ice-cream. (He had been influenced in favour of Italian-style meals since they'd had a holiday in

Verona and he'd learned what Italian football stars tended to eat, at least according to feature articles in the press.)

'But something's worrying you,' she remarked. 'I do know the signs, Sam. Is it anything you can share or do you have to sort it out on your own?'

'Well,' he said at last, sitting down in an easy chair and sipping from a glass of mineral water with ice and lemon, 'it's the Todd boy, Alex. Got so much going for him but won't just stick with that. Must get on the wrong side of the ref or some opponent and cause no end of trouble. Had to take him off in the end, otherwise we could've finished up with ten players. Then, just as I knew he would, he sulked. Typical.'

'So I suppose you'll drop him for a couple of matches until he sees things your way,' his wife said with the certainty of someone who knew precisely what her partner thinks and how he reacts to situations.

But he shook his head. 'Not too sure about that. The boy scores goals, I've got to give him that. Really knows where the net is. He got two for us today and he might have had more but for getting tangled up with one of their defenders. Should've walked away but he can't do that. Not at present, anyway. Hence taking him off for his own and the team's good.'

'So . . .'

'So you know as well as I do, Rina, that goal-getters don't grow on trees. The best are a very special breed and young Todd might be one of 'em one day. *If* we can sort him out.'

'Why don't you discuss it with his dad? I mean, Ricky Todd is keen enough on the team, isn't he? Likes to get involved. So can't he see that Alex needs to control his temper?'

'You'd think so because he seems an intelligent man. After all, he runs his own successful business, he's responsible for a whole range of people with different emotions and temperaments. But when it comes down to his own son I think he's only concerned for the present, not the future. When it comes to matches he's always urging Alex to get stuck in, to beat 'em at their own game as he likes to put it. Quite a forceful type himself, Ricky Todd, I imagine. Don't think I'd care to work in his factory.'

'But that shouldn't prevent you from suggesting he helps Alex get a grip on his temper – for the good of the team,' Mrs Saxton pointed out.

'True, true. If he comes along to the training session on Tuesday evening I can tackle him then. Have to, otherwise the situation will get worse, I'm sure of it.'

'Do many parents turn up at training these days? I mean, they don't seem to bother to turn out for school events, meetings that are vitally concerned with their own children's education. The Head's thoroughly disappointed by most people's indifference to what's happening in the classroom.'

'It varies,' Sam told her. 'Some weeks there's only the players and a few hangers-on, boys who'd like to play for us but simply aren't good enough. But most weeks parents are there. I *do* encourage them to share in the team's progress, don't I? And there shouldn't be anything to hide at training. So everyone's welcome. Of course, some of the boys themselves don't like to see parents present. Not their own, anyway!' He paused and then added reflectively: 'Though I wouldn't say that applies to Alex. He likes to turn it on when his dad's there. At those times he's even more desperate than usual to get the man-of-the-match award, if that's possible. Seems to think he deserves it *every* match whether he's been in good form or otherwise. No sense of what's right and wrong, that boy. No judgement, that's his trouble: what's fair and what's definitely unfair.'

'Well, I can tell he won't be receiving the award for this match,' remarked his wife, pouring herself a glass of white wine and taking a first appreciative sip. 'You're going to make one of your surprise choices again, are you?'

Gently Sam shook his head, though not in disagreement with her. 'Just haven't decided yet, that's all. I don't know why you think they're "surprise" choices. I just feel that it's a good idea sometimes to give the award to a lad who isn't expecting it because he didn't do anything special. It should be there for encouragement, that's the thing. *Encouraging* players is what coaching's all about.' Then he added reflectively, 'Or should be.'

His wife smiled. 'Well, let me encourage you to sit down now, forget all about football for a few minutes and enjoy your food. It may be the only award *you* get today.'

Lloyd had the door open even before the car braked sharply to a stop in the small park on top of the cliff. The football was already under one arm and when he drop-kicked it his aim was a sturdy metal waste bin by the footpath. It was just as well he managed to hit the target for otherwise the ball would surely have sailed over the edge of the cliff to the sands far below. He raced to collect the rebound.

'Lloyd!' his mother yelled. 'Don't rush off. We're going to eat first. You can have your kick-around later.'

He didn't respond, though he knew she wouldn't give up and she did have a very loud voice when she needed it. Allowing the ball to come back at him from another shot at the waste bin, he then stepped over it, spun round in a complete circle and tried to flick it upwards so that he could volley it as far as possible, a distance at least as wide as a soccer pitch. Unfortunately, he got tangled up in his own gyrations and sat down heavily on the tarmac.

'Lloyd!' his mother yelled. 'Get up! I haven't money to spare for new trousers because you've ruined them sitting down on the tarmac.'

The indignity of what had happened to him as well as the public admission of poverty impelled him to get to his feet and glance round quickly to see if anyone was listening. Fortunately, the park was almost deserted; but then, it was most people's lunch-time and it really wasn't a warm enough day to sit about in the open. He thought he might have twisted his knee and he walked gingerly until he realized his mother was watching carefully. It wouldn't do to appear injured so he tossed the ball into the air and then tried to trap it on the first bounce. Sadly, he made a hash of that, too, and the ball squirted away.

'Look, I want something to eat even if you don't, so –'

'OK, so let's go down to the beach and eat there,' Lloyd interrupted her, thinking that soft sand would be easier to play on at present. 'Then I –'

'NO!' Serena Colmer insisted. 'These picnic tables here are for people to use so we're sure going to use them. We'll eat in a civilized fashion. We won't be getting sand in our sandwiches.'

'There's already sand in sandwiches, Mum. Just think about the spelling!' he pointed out delightedly.

'All right, Bright Boy, all right, I'll give you that one. But we're sitting here all the same. We're going to gaze at the sea and become calm inside. We'll talk about that little holiday we're going to take at Christmas with your aunt and uncle in London. So, SIT!'

Lloyd said, 'Woof, woof!' and then turned round and round in a tight circle like a dog chasing its own tail. But that sent twinges through his knee again so he sat down at the table and tried to look perfectly at home.

'Don't know where you get the energy from, not me, that's for sure,' his mum remarked, setting out the sandwiches and scones and cans of soft drinks with plastic beakers beside them. 'Now eat, Lloyd.'

'This is what gives me energy,' he told her, biting happily into a tuna-with-mayonnaise double-decker. 'And football gives me a buzz. It's the best thing in the world. You'll see that, Mum, when I'm playing in the World Cup. You'll be real glad you always fed me energy food. You'll be able to take the credit. Fact is, I'll mention it when those guys with TV cameras come and interview me about scoring the winning goal in the Final. Mum, you'll get lots of folk coming up to you afterwards, saying how lucky you are to have a son as brilliant as me!'

She laughed. 'Tell you one thing, Lloyd, you don't lack confidence, that's for sure. With an imagination like yours it won't matter if you don't do everything you think you're going to. Your brain will convince you you did it anyway.'

As he finished one sandwich and selected the next (cheese and pickled walnut) his grin faded. 'But I don't think I'm convincing Sam the Slammer that I'm good enough at present,' he murmured. 'I mean, he's not always picking me to start the match like he did today. I never know until I get to the game whether I'm playing. And even when I do something really good he doesn't say much, doesn't heap praise on me like with Danny or Alex.

'I mean, Sam almost goes crazy with happiness when Danny does something just ordinary like tipping the ball over the bar or jumping out to catch it from a corner kick. Makes me wonder if I ought to be a goalkeeper instead of a midfielder.'

He was about to toss away a hard crust when, as if on cue, a seagull came swooping low over his head. So Lloyd flung the bread upwards and before it had time to drop again the bird changed direction and seized its reward. Lloyd, impressed, clapped his hands and then flung it another titbit.

'Just like a goalkeeper – makes one catch and everybody cheers,' he remarked.

His mother, who'd been pondering his remarks about Danny, enquired, 'Is your goalie the coach's favourite player, then? Does he get special favours?'

Lloyd shook his head. 'No, I can't say that. Don't think Sam really has any proper favourites. Says he treats us all alike.'

'And does he, does he *really*?' Mrs Colmer persisted. Because she was a single parent it often went through her mind that Lloyd needed a father figure, someone he could turn to when necessary, someone who genuinely cared about Lloyd, his present and his future. She had wondered whether Sam Saxton might fulfil that role in Lloyd's life but she had no idea whether he was capable of it.

'Yeah, I think so,' her son replied after thinking about it. 'There's nobody he really goes for – you know, praising all the time, doing favours for. With Danny it's just, well, Sam says if your goalie's reliable he gives a lift to the whole team. So he keeps telling Danny he's brilliant to *make* him brilliant. Doesn't always work, though. Sometimes Dan gets a bit too cocky and then he can make terrible mistakes.'

He glanced at his mum but she was simply looking thoughtful. So he continued in a wistful vein, 'Wish he *did* go in for favourites 'cos then he might choose me! Don't know why he would, but you never know. He might. Still, I wouldn't mind if he just thought I deserved a man-of-the-match award now and again.'

'I'm sure he will,' his mum replied with one of her million-wattage smiles. 'Nobody could try harder than you, Lloyd. So –'

Swallowing the last of his sandwich, he jumped to his feet and seized the ball. 'OK, let's go. Down to the beach. I've got to try harder with my shooting. Mum, you could be my goalkeeper and –'

'No way!' she said, still laughing. 'I'm totally the wrong shape for that. You *know* I can't catch a ball to save my life. But I'm sure your shooting'll improve.'

'Wish I was as sure as you are,' Lloyd murmured to himself as he sprinted towards the winding path that led down to the beach.

2 Training Methods

'Go, go, GO!' the coach yelled at them and
the players hared away as if hounds from hell
were snapping at their heels. They ran to the
cone, touched it for luck, and then sprinted
back to their starting point. Then the next
boy in line dashed away in the same frantic
fashion.

Sam Saxton nodded approvingly, glancing
from time to time at the stop-watch he held
in the palm of his hand. He wasn't actually
timing anything his players were doing but
he believed they'd work harder if they
thought they were competing against the
clock. In the shadowy light falling on the all-
weather pitch at the village leisure centre, the
few spectators, resting squad members and
three bored-looking parents, looked frozen.
Most of them envied the runners. Ricky Todd,
however, wasn't among them. Standing alone

beside a goal-post he was watching everything through narrowed eyes and occasionally shook his head as if baffled by what he was witnessing.

'Come on, Foggy, put more effort into it, son!' Sam called to a round-faced, fair-haired boy wearing an all-red track suit that was completely different from everyone else's kit this evening.

'I *am* going as fast as I can,' Marc Thrale protested, though not too forcefully. 'I'm a bit tired, actually. I mean, we had football at school today and I played a blinder. So I don't have quite the same energy as usual, Sam.'

The coach gave him a thoughtful look from under the lowered peak of his favourite baseball cap. Usually Foggy gave 100 per cent in training as he did in a match; and usually, too, he was direct and honest in everything he did. He was a boy who had an almost desperate desire to get to the top in football, though Sam reckoned Marc had severe limitations in real skills on the ball. But there was just something in his present manner which suggested to the Kings' coach that this time he wasn't being strictly honest.

'So who were you playing today, Foggy?' he asked casually.

'Oh, er, nobody special. Just a big kick-around, really. But organized. We all played hard, Sam, really hard.'

'I see.' Plainly, that meant he didn't; but it was one of his conversational punctuation marks. 'Well, I wouldn't want you exhausting yourself, Foggy. I need fit players, *super*-fit players, especially when you're playing in a team against a side like Clocklane. Teams don't come much fitter than them, I can tell you. So if you're going to make my team for next Sunday, Foggy, well . . .'

'Sam, I was just taking a breather, that's all!' Foggy assured him hastily. 'If I try, I can out-run everybody here, no danger. Just you watch!'

By this time most of the other runners had eased off, partly because they were listening to the exchange between Sam and Foggy. So when Foggy broke into a dramatic sprint, as if he were attempting a world record, he had no trouble at all in overtaking Alex and Lloyd who were ahead of him.

'See!' he chortled. 'Told you I could. That's

because I'm the fittest player on the park. And the fittest should always be captain of the team, shouldn't he?'

Sam Saxton wasn't rising to that old bait again but he didn't have to because at that moment Ricky Todd decided it was time to say what he'd wanted to say for a long time. He saw that Alex was trying to catch his eye but he ignored him. This definitely wasn't the moment for his son to intervene.

'Sam, good to see you again,' he greeted him genially, rather as if he were trying to impress a business acquaintance or potential customer at his furniture factory. 'I always like the atmosphere you create at training sessions.'

'Thanks,' Sam replied briefly, taking the proffered hand and wondering what might be coming next. Alex's dad wasn't the sort to engage in chit-chat in the middle of training. He supposed it would be about Alex's version at home of why he'd been substituted against the Hawks two days earlier. Well, he could answer that if Ricky Todd were prepared to listen to someone else's opinion instead of just his own.

'You know, I agree with you totally, *totally*, about getting our boys as fit as possible. Got to compete on at least level terms, haven't we?' Ricky remarked with one of his business-winning smiles. Sam said nothing because he knew this was merely an opening shot before he aimed at his chief target.

'But I do think also that players need at least as much ballwork as fitness exercises,' Mr Todd went on smoothly. 'Some of them, *most* of them, I reckon need it more. After all, schools and families do their best to keep children in good health these days, make sure they eat the right kind of food. That sort of thing. But ballwork, well, that's *vital* if they're going to be good enough to beat any team they meet.'

He stopped at that point, eyebrows raised, waiting for Sam's comment. But the Kings' coach didn't say anything for a few moments. Then, when Ricky didn't continue, he gave a kind of half-shrug and asked: 'So what're you saying, then?'

Ricky tried to remain cheerful. 'I thought the point was obvious, Sam. That we should be doing more work *with* the ball. Now.

Tonight. Before the boys are too tired to make the most of the training session. As Marc reminded us, these youngsters have already put in a hard day's work at school. They haven't got limitless energy, you know.'

Alex seemed about to say something but his father held up an imperious hand to prevent any unwelcome interruption. The only person Ricky wanted to hear from was Sam Saxton.

'I know all that, otherwise I wouldn't be the coach,' Sam replied in a very matter-of-fact manner. 'I've worked with boys of this age long enough to know a good deal about their stamina and fitness. And I also know that ballwork is vital; of course I do. But I believe body fitness comes first. Without that there's not much point in trying to control a ball.'

Ricky nodded vigorously. 'I go along with all that, Sam. It's just that, well, time's getting on and I reckon some sharp work on the ball would work wonders with the squad. It'd be a shot in the arm. Give them something to *enjoy*. Fitness training on its own can be a bit of a bore.'

'Dead right, Dad!' exclaimed Alex before his father could quell him. But then, he had plenty of support because Marc and Lloyd and several of the other players were nodding enthusiastically.

'We're getting round to it, we'll be working with the ball in a minute or two,' Sam conceded while still wondering when Ricky would raise the matter of the substitution which was surely the real reason for his visit to the training session this evening. 'We're going to practise defending at corners and set-pieces. Something that's been worrying me lately. We've just got to be a lot tighter at those times.'

'But we did that *last* week, and the week before,' Marc Thrale complained. Because he was a midfielder who liked to think of himself as an extra forward he felt such matters didn't really involve him.

'Well, those lessons weren't learned thoroughly so we've got to do 'em again until we get it right,' Sam pointed out sharply. There was some criticism he could've made of Marc's own contributions, or lack of them, in that area but he wouldn't do it in front of parents. Although neither Marc's mum nor his dad was present he was well aware how his comments were often passed on by other adults for a variety of reasons.

Ricky guessed that Alex, too, would have the same reservations about defending but he wasn't going to say anything that could be interpreted as petty. But before he could make any remark at all, a woman who'd arrived silently beside him said eagerly, 'Oh, good! That will help Kieren. He keeps worrying about his positioning in defence.'

'Oh, er, glad to hear that, Jakki,' Sam told her. 'I'm forever telling them all that they should think about their football all the time, not just when they're on the pitch. It may be too late then to do the right thing. But if you keep *thinking* about your game, well, you should develop an instinct for doing the *correct* thing.'

Ricky glanced at the small, blonde-haired woman beside him. All he really knew about her was that she was the mother of Kieren Kelly, a fairly thin and tall boy who wasn't a regular member of the team. Now Kieren was standing on the edge of the group of players awaiting their next instruction and, not surprisingly, he wasn't looking pleased with her intervention. While Sam went off to organize his squad into attackers and defenders for the promised ballwork, Ricky smiled at Mrs Kelly and said, 'Don't often see you at training. Are you developing a keenness for the game or something?' Of course, he didn't mention that he wasn't a regular spectator, either.

'Well, Kieren's becoming almost fanatical about his football, talks about it endlessly, probably even dreams about it most of the night. But he seems worried, too, whenever a match comes up. Maybe lack of confidence or something like that, possibly he's even afraid of the coach. I mean, Sam Saxton does exert a powerful influence on his players, doesn't he?'

'Certainly does,' Ricky agreed, still smiling. He thought he could detect where Kieren might get some of his worries from. 'Sometimes some of us worry that he, er, puts too much pressure on the boys. On the other hand, most of them want to get to the top in soccer, don't they? Play for star teams and so on. Is Kieren like that?'

'Goodness, I hope not!' The worry lines were now deeply etched on her face. 'I mean, I'm sure he doesn't consider himself anywhere near good enough to reach that level. That's an impossible dream, I imagine. But it doesn't stop him from wanting to do well with the Kings. Oh, and I think he's also a bit bothered about this German boy who's coming to stay with us. How they'll get on together, whether they really have anything in common.'

'Oh, I didn't know about that,' Ricky said in a tone that conveyed he'd be perfectly happy to hear more.

'Well, I don't suppose many people do. It's just that *I* keep thinking about it because I have the job of making sure Karl-Heinz is happy and doesn't feel homesick and so on.'

When she paused Ricky, grinning, asked: 'Let me guess: that must be Karl with a "K" and not a "C". Right?'

'Well, yes, but what – oh, I *see*. Another "K" in our lives! Even my sister said the other day that we scatter "K's" around like confetti at a wedding. I mean, even Clark, my husband, has a "K" in his name. So, yes, that's the way to spell Karl-Heinz. I just hope he likes football because otherwise he'll not get much out of Kieren. So the visit could be a real disaster.'

'Oh, so you don't know the boy, then? Or, at least, not very well?' Ricky was happy to keep the conversation going because it was too soon to say to Sam Saxton what else was in his mind. He felt he should do a little discreet observing first.

'No, not really. Although he's German he actually lives in France because that's where his dad runs a restaurant. He doesn't see much of his mother as his parents are divorced and his mum has remarried. Anyway, Karl-Heinz's dad has sold his old restaurant and is about to open a new one. That's why it's not easy for him to have Karl-Heinz around at present. He wants to get the business launched properly. So, well, I offered him a break over here for two or three weeks. I mean, he's learning English at school so the experience ought to be good for him.'

'I see,' Ricky murmured. 'So is the boy's father a friend of yours?'

Jakki Kelly looked a little embarrassed and

slightly pink as she dealt with that last question. 'Er, yes, you could say that, I suppose. I met him years ago but – oh, well, that's really an old story. The thing is my husband and I have eaten at his restaurant several times but without actually meeting Karl-Heinz. Wonderful food, wonderful.' She switched her attention to the play and was rewarded instantly by seeing Kieren head the ball firmly out of play for another corner. 'Oh, well done, Kieren! Good header!'

Ricky forebore to tell her that the coach wouldn't think much of the header. All Kieren had succeeded in doing was giving the other side an advantage. Alex, he noticed, was standing idly on the edge of the box, taking neither part nor interest in the proceedings. It was time for Ricky to make his next suggestion. Politely he excused himself to Jakki and then sprinted on to the pitch.

Sam was just applauding Danny Loxham, the goalkeeper, for a particularly athletic save from a close-range hooked shot when Ricky reached the edge of the penalty area. 'This time we'll try a new defensive wall, try to spread out a bit more to lengthen it,' he was suggesting. 'It might be a good thing for Danny to get a chance to see who's actually taking the free kick. So –'

'Sam, sorry to butt in, but could I just ask something?' Ricky said loudly. 'Couldn't we have something else going on with another ball? I see there is a spare one over there. In fact, if we got out another ball as well we could do some dribbling or speed-passing skills.'

'Hey, great idea!' Lloyd enthused, although none of the other boys said a word.

Sam's frown was fierce. 'Ricky, we're already doing what you wanted, developing ball skills. Defending is just as important as attacking. I'm sure even Alex would agree with that. You must have heard me say to Jakki that we've got to get things right at corners and free kicks. I'm trying to perfect that, all right?'

It wasn't really a question, just Sam's way of implying that he knew best, so don't argue. Ricky, however, was never easily diverted from his chosen course in anything. 'OK, fine, but while you're dealing with that I could take a few of the boys for the other stuff. Honestly, I'd be happy to do it. Help to keep me fit, too!' He laughed but didn't win any response from the coach. 'So I'll grab that ball over there. Have we got another one handy?'

Sam shook his head. 'We've got what you can see. We don't have any spare balls.'

To their credit none of the boys laughed aloud but their expressions said everything. Kieren glanced at his mum but she didn't appear to be listening, anyway.

'But Sam, if there's any shortage of equipment you know you only have to ask any of us on the Supporters' Committee,' Ricky pointed out gently but firmly. 'You know we're always willing to raise more cash if it's needed.'

The coach closed his eyes for a moment. Parent power, as he thought of it, was always a threat to his authority but it hadn't previously come forward at night-time training. Perhaps that was only because so few of the boys' parents, or step-parents, attended. He'd believed Ricky Todd was there this evening simply to talk about Alex's conduct and attitude. Now he suspected Ricky's offer to help with the coaching and his targeting of an alleged lack of equipment was his way of undermining Sam's position. Because all he wanted to do at present was concentrate on his training ideas he wasn't quite sure how to deal with this manoeuvre.

'Look, we cope most of the time, so it's not a problem,' he said brusquely. 'If you don't mind, I'd like to get on with what we're doing. I can't keep these boys out too late. You should know that. Most of the parents would soon protest if I did.'

'Of course, of course, you're right, Sam,' Ricky said pacifyingly. 'OK if I just do a bit with the ball over there? Won't interfere with your work, I promise.'

'Help yourself,' the coach replied, hoping he didn't sound too grudging.

Ricky wasn't sure who he ought to take with him but when he jerked his head at Alex the gesture was interpreted by Marc and Lloyd and Josh Rowley as an invitation to them, too. So they scampered across to the other side of the pitch when Ricky hooked the ball in that direction. He sensed that some of the defenders, including Kieren Kelly, would also have liked to join in but they daren't desert the official coach.

'So what're you going to do, Dad?' Alex wanted to know. 'I mean, are you going to give us a demonstration?'

It was a serious question and until that moment Ricky hadn't worked out exactly what he would do. If he'd assumed anything it was that he'd pick up ideas from what Sam was doing. Then he noticed the bright white and orange cones on the edge of the pitch and inspiration arrived instantly.

'We'll set those up at intervals and I want you all to dribble in between them, getting from one end of the line to the other as fast as possible without allowing the ball to touch any of the cones,' he instructed. 'But – and listen to this – you must use only the *left* foot. The right's just to run with!'

With only one ball available the boys had to take it in turn. Predictably, Alex wanted to go first and, equally predictably, he had to show off; but because he was able to use both feet he made few mistakes. So Ricky was able to praise him without any sense of prejudice. He wished he could congratulate Josh on his performance but the tall boy with the short, curly hair was surprisingly clumsy even when he resorted to steering the ball with his right foot. Until now Ricky hadn't taken much notice of Josh, although everyone remarked on the brevity of his shorts.

'Don't worry about it, son, just do your best, you're getting there,' Ricky tried to encourage him. 'Not everybody gets it right the first time. Just relax. You'll do it.'

Why he'd called Josh 'son' he couldn't imagine, except that it was a form of address favoured by many coaches. So, Ricky reflected, perhaps that's why I did it: I *am* thinking like a coach. That cheered him greatly.

'Right, boys,' he said when he thought they'd had enough of that, 'let's get into something else. This is a game called Tiger-Ball and I played it when I was your age. Improves your passing skills no end *and* helps to sharpen up your interceptions. We use the centre circle and one of you stands right on the centre spot, the rest spread out around the edge of the circle. What you do is pass the ball to somebody else, whoever you like, but not to the one right next to you. To start with we use only the left foot; we'll switch to the right later. And the player in the middle tries like mad to intercept the ball. He'll often succeed if he can anticipate where the pass is going. OK? You'll see what I mean when we get going. Don't look so worried, Josh! It's not as complicated as maybe I made it sound. You'll get the hang of it in no time.'

They were much more disciplined than he'd expected. When he reprimanded Marc for trying to lob the ball above head height instead of passing it along the ground the boy immediately apologized and looked genuinely contrite. Of all the players he was the one who surprised and most impressed the new assistant coach.

Ricky hadn't been aware that Marc possessed so much control and could move so quickly. In the past, Sam Saxton had often been critical of Marc, pointing out that he needed 'to think and act faster'. Well, he was a different player in this situation and when it was his turn to go into the middle he won the ball back almost immediately with a lightning interception. Under the rules of the game he therefore rejoined those passing the ball to each other while Josh, who'd delivered the pass Marc seized upon, had to replace him in the middle. And Josh, again, didn't perform well: he didn't get anywhere near an interception. But perhaps, Ricky reasoned, Josh was tiring faster than the others; after all, with those long legs of his he'd probably outgrown his strength.

'Well done, well done,' he signalled, calling a halt to the proceedings and then slapping each of them on the back. 'You worked really hard and showed lots of good touches.'

'It was great, Dad, really enjoyed it,' Alex declared and the others joined in, sounding equally enthusiastic.

'Sure I didn't give you a hard time?' he asked Marc a trifle anxiously.

'No, no, Mr Todd, I needed that. I mean, I want to get better and better,' Marc assured him so earnestly that Ricky couldn't doubt his words.

Jakki Kelly, who'd drifted across to watch him at work, smiled warmly as he turned towards her. 'That was really good,' she told him. 'You're a natural. Sam the Slammer had better watch out for his job!'

'Wish I could've been over here hitting passes like that,' said Kieren, who'd come to join them now that the training session was officially over for everyone. 'Don't think I learned much from all that defending stuff. Too much like a chess match. You can't work everything out in advance at soccer, can you, Mr Todd?'

'Er, no, quite right, Kieren,' he responded cautiously, hoping Sam hadn't overheard that exchange. The coach's expression was impossible to read so far as Ricky was concerned. But he felt the need to say something about the events of the evening. Unhappily, he chose the wrong subject.

'Going back to what I said earlier, Sam, I'll be very happy to buy some more footballs for the boys to use,' he offered. 'I mean, that way we don't have to wait for the Committee to raise the money first. I'd like to help.'

'Me, too,' said Jakki Kelly unexpectedly. 'Kieren gets a lot out of his football with the Kings so I'm very willing to put something back, just like Ricky here.'

Before Ricky could even turn to smile his

appreciation of this support Sam snapped, 'No thanks. Good of you to offer. But I'm quite happy with the way things are going. We've really got all the equipment we need for the present.'

'Oh,' said Ricky, because there wasn't much else he could say after such a rebuff. He glanced at Jakki and suspected she was a little embarrassed, understandably.

'Tell him about me being subbed on Sunday,' Alex whispered, but loud enough for Sam to hear. 'You said you would, Dad.'

'Now's not the time – later, maybe,' Ricky replied in a low tone. His mind was full of other matters he might raise with the Kings' coach but he sensed it really was the wrong time to talk about them with Sam in such a defensive, if not aggressive, mood. The next match, though, seemed a safe topic.

'Have you got any special plans for the game against Clocklane, then, Sam?' he enquired in a friendly manner. 'The Highlea Knock-out Cup is a highly desirable prize, isn't it?'

'Oh, yes, good one – highly Highlea!' Marc chortled. His booming voice carried so far that people way down the street turned to see what was going on. Nobody associated with the Kings ever had to wonder why he was popularly known as Foghorn.

'Every competition we're in is highly desirable to win as you put it,' Sam responded, sounding a little sour. 'You must know by now, Ricky, that I pick the team I believe will win the game for us.'

'Of course, of course, Sam, but, well, lots of experts think one-off games in Cups are different from League games. I mean, defences win marathon contests, don't they, while attackers win Cup-ties?'

'That is a theory I've heard about, yes,' was all Sam would commit himself to; and Ricky decided it wasn't worth trying to take the argument any further. For one thing, the boys who were still in their company were listening avidly, possibly sensing a row between the coach and the top striker's dad. Well, that wouldn't do any of them any good, Ricky knew. For the time being, at least, the official coach was entitled to full support from players and supporters alike.

'OK, then, Sam, see you at the next game.

I enjoyed tonight's work-out,' Ricky said, steering Alex across the road towards the short cut that led to their home.

'Goodnight, Ricky, Alex. And, er, thanks for your help with the training,' Sam added rather grudgingly.

'Alex, d'you think you'll be in the team against Clocklane?' Lloyd, trailing along beside them, wanted to know. It was in his mind that he would like to try his luck at being a striker all the time if there was a definite place for him in the team. These days, though, he could never be sure until the day of the game whether he would be playing or sitting on the bench or left out completely. The answer he received, however, didn't provide any encouragement.

'I'd better be – or else . . .' Alex muttered fiercely.

3 Sensation!

The rain was pelting down as if it would never cease as the Goal Kings' minibus swung into the car-park behind the club-house of the Clocklane ground where everything looked tidy and the pitch itself was surrounded by a low-level, white-painted wooden rail. But the weather was doing its best to ruin the playing surface and already small pools were expanding in the goalmouths and the centre circle.

'They'll never play in this, will they?' Karen Rowley said to Ricky Todd as they clambered out of the bus and experienced the strength of the downpour. 'I mean, look at the mud! Mud drains strength out of young bodies, you know, when they have to plough through that sort of stuff. I don't think Josh'll like it one bit.'

'Well, it's the same for everybody, you

know. Mud's a great leveller, that's what they all say. Trouble is, it'll bring us down to Clocklane's level. Our superior skills won't count for as much.'

'Well, I can tell *you* think the game'll go ahead,' Karen snorted.

'It's just got to, unless conditions are really impossible,' Ricky replied. 'It's a Cup-tie and therefore the organizers need to keep everything on the move so that every team plays at the same time. A back-log of fixtures would be a disaster. It's also why they don't go in for replays. Instead they have a penalty shoot-out if the scores are level at the end of normal time. They've got to get a result, a winner from each tie. So . . .'

'And the Final's in the New Year, so we can get our hands on a trophy and some medals *miles* before the end of the season,' Alex rejoiced. 'And we *are* going to win the Cup, no danger, just so long as I get scoring chances.'

Sam Saxton looked as if he didn't believe anybody would be winning anything today if the weather didn't relent. His gloom matched the clouds and Ricky couldn't help wondering what advice the coach would be giving his players. If he himself were in charge he would order the Kings to attack ferociously from the outset and be determined to score as many goals as possible, not worrying if they conceded one so long as they scored at least two. His argument was that the longer the game went on the harder it would be to score at all because the cloying mud would sap players' energies. In the later stages a defensive wall would be harder than ever to breach.

Sam, however, was saying nothing at all within earshot of spectators, many of whom were huddling under umbrellas or trying to cram into the tiny stand in front of the half-way line. Quickly the coach herded the Kings into the changing-room which, when he was in charge, was always out of bounds to parents and supporters and other non-players. He was even reluctant to admit a physio or doctor unless their presence was absolutely essential. He'd already had a word with the ref and so knew the game would start even though Sam himself doubted it would run its full course.

'I don't need to tell you that it's going to be tough out there,' he said as the boys changed into their playing kit. He always wandered around as he spoke, and his voice was deliberately low, but they all listened because they never knew who he would turn to for a personal word.

'You can all see what it's like, so the thing to remember is to *take care*, don't *rush* into anything if you can avoid it. I know a football flies around at a fast rate but it won't travel so fast today. The mud'll hold it up. Keeping your feet is important. I've checked your boots and you've all got a good stud-length, so that'll help. Above all, try to be calm. Won't be easy, but try. For my sake. For the team's sake. For the Kings!'

It was his most familiar rallying cry and they rather liked to hear him say it. They were all, every single one of them, desperately keen to win a medal, to have something to hold and then proudly display in their bedrooms, something that *proved* they were true winners. None of them, so far, had won anything more significant than a man-of-the-match award and that wasn't enough; that was just domestic and they felt the need to let everyone in the village of Rodale Kings, and much further afield if possible, know how good and successful a team they were.

'I don't want to be subbing you today, Alex,' Sam told his chief striker. 'You're in the team on merit. Keep it that way, right to the final whistle, OK?'

'Don't worry, I'll get the goals today, Sam!' Alex declared, grinning hugely. From the moment the team had been announced Alex had burned to score, to match the hat-trick he was sure he'd've registered against the Hawks. Well, today he was going to go one better: never in his life had he hit a four-timer. Today, he vowed to himself, he was going to do it. Best thing of all, his dad was here to see it.

'Do your best,' the coach said to the majority of his players, patting each one on the shoulder as they filed out of the changing-room. But for two of them he reserved an individual comment.

'You're the rock, Joe,' he said softly to his central defender. 'Just let the waves of their attacks crash on you. Then they'll be harmless.'

'Sure thing, Boss,' replied the boy with the surprisingly hunched shoulders and a nose dented from the only game of rugby he'd ever played. Joe Parbold believed that Sam really liked being called 'Boss' because he never shrugged it aside. Usually he smiled when he heard it and Joe also took comfort that the Boss hardly ever criticized him even after he'd made a clumsy tackle or a bad pass.

'Keep concentrating, Danny,' urged Sam, keeping his last words of all for his keeper, the player most of the boys recognized as Sam's favourite. But they didn't resent that because Danny Loxham really was good at his job. When he let in a goal usually it was only because it had been impossible for him to prevent it. Danny hardly needed to be reminded to concentrate. Throughout a match he never stopped moving, dancing along the goal-line, pacing back and forth across the box, jumping up and down to try to touch the crossbar, performing, back-arching and knees-bend exercises, leaping out to punch the air as if it were an invisible ball. Yet his concentration never seemed to waver. It was no wonder that Sam Saxton saw

Danny as a future star in some Premiership side.

'Their forwards are big guys, they'll use their weight, so expect a rough old time,' Sam added. But Danny merely nodded. He tended to treat all assaults on his goalmouth with the same determination and flair. He wasn't completely fearless but he liked to give the impression he was.

In their tangerine shirts and yellow shorts, Clocklane Strikers were distinctive and colourful and as they came on to the pitch someone near the dug-out began to ring out a kind of tune on chiming bells.

'Well, that's original – good for them,' remarked Karen Rowley, who was trying to cheer up while wondering how Josh, who insisted on wearing so little during a game, would fare in these saturating conditions.

'They don't strike terror into me, though!' joked Marc Thrale who was passing the huddle of Kings' supporters at that moment.

'Sounds like the boys are in the best of spirits, anyway,' said Ricky, who'd been hoping that Jakki Kelly would turn up. There was something he was anxious to talk to her about because he believed they were on the same wavelength.

The game began sensationally. From the kick-off the Strikers chased upfield almost to a man as if they'd all been made aware of Ricky's private thoughts about the importance of grabbing an early goal. In fact, their own coach had recommended an identical approach believing that his heavyweight forwards could prove irresistible in the mud. Even Foggy Thrale, normally strong in the tackle when he went for the ball in determined fashion, was brushed easily aside as he attempted to gain possession. Clocklane's leading goal-scorer, Marcus, who seemed to be all elbows and knees as he roared forward, yelled for a return pass immediately after surrendering the ball to outwit a challenge. And when he got it he looked up, reckoned he could hit the target from that distance, and fired the ball towards the top right-hand corner of the net.

Danny Loxham wasn't the sort of goal-keeper to be caught out of position from that range. His alertness had shown him just how stretched out the opposition were. So, the moment the ball was in his hands, he drop-kicked it as far as he could manage, but aiming it towards Dominic Allenby. Dominic, who always preferred to play as an attacker but had been allotted a midfield role by Sam for this match, played his part perfectly, too.

'Yours, Alex!' he yelled, sweeping the ball instantaneously between two Clocklane defenders for his team-mate to run on to; and Alex, anticipating a pass, was already on the move.

'Go for it, Alex!' he heard his dad yell. But Alex didn't need telling anything. He was convinced he was going to score.

Because of the speed of Alex's reactions he was clear of what defence remained to protect Clocklane's goalkeeper. Stranded by the surge upfield of most of his team-mates he had no option but to come out and pray the one-on-one situation would end in his favour. In his experience, most strikers suffered a loss of nerve when bearing down on goal with only the keeper to beat. Sometimes it seemed so easy to them to score and they hesitated, just momentarily. But, usually, fatally.

Alex wasn't in that category. His nerves

remained as strong as ever as he took the ball up to his opponent, jinked to go one way, swerved in the opposite direction and, with his left foot, dragged the ball out of the goalkeeper's reach even if he dived full-length. He would have been clear with the empty goal ahead of him and a certain scorer if the keeper hadn't, in his desperate attempt to prevent a goal, grabbed Alex's right ankle and sent him sprawling.

'Penalty!' yelled Alex, rolling to his feet in practically the same movement as he'd gone down. And there couldn't possibly be any doubt it would be awarded, although equally naturally the Strikers' coach was shaking his head fiercely in disbelief that one of his players could be punished. Sam Saxton was showing no emotion at all, while Ricky couldn't restrain himself from punching the air with approval. But then, when he saw the referee was merely brandishing a yellow card, his mood changed.

'Should be a red one – makes me see red, that does,' he declared to anyone who would listen. 'That was a professional foul if ever there was one. Stopped a definite goal. So the offender has to go, right?'

Karen Rowley, who turned to find that Ricky was trying to get her opinion, just shrugged. It seemed to her that the rain was getting heavier, if possible, and this game really shouldn't be allowed to go on any longer. She was sure she wouldn't be the only one who'd like to get home to some warm clothing and a hot drink.

Alex had grabbed the ball as soon as he was on his feet and wasn't going to relinquish it until he'd converted the penalty. There wasn't a shred of doubt in his mind he'd get his revenge on the goalie by slamming the ball past him. Normally Joe Parbold would take penalties but Alex would insist it was his kick. After all, he'd earned it. Joe, however, wasn't inclined to argue; he had complete confidence in Alex's shooting from the spot.

He was right: the ball positively whistled past the dejected goalie and into the top of the net. Alex leapt into the air in his delight and spoilt the effect only by slipping on a particularly greasy patch of mud as he landed. Ricky was clapping loudly, hands high above his head, but Karen couldn't bring herself to do more than whisper, 'Well done!' She couldn't help wishing it was Josh who'd scored. Getting a goal for the Kings in a Cup-tie was his private version of heaven, she suspected.

That first-minute set-back didn't restrain Clocklane from attacking in force again from the kick-off. Their coach had already conveyed a message to his team via the captain: 'Hit back right away. We can't afford to be a goal down.'

Sam was doing some semaphoring of his own as Marcus, in possession again, tried to bustle past Joe and Foggy. His signals were directed at Dominic: plainly he wanted him to drop back to reinforce the defence. If the Kings could hold out for the next few minutes it would then be the time to try to add to their lead. Drilled by Sam for weeks to deal with situations like this, defenders conceded ground or hit the ball out anywhere so long as the opposition didn't get a shot on goal.

'Come on, boys, they're wide open for a counter-attack,' Ricky was calling. 'Get the ball up to our strikers.'

Sam, hearing everything, frowned but didn't speak. He attempted to catch Dominic's attention, to move him to a more central position, but Dominic, quite sensibly, was shadowing Clocklane's most elusive player, a winger who was keeping to the drier patches of the pitch. Alex was patrolling the half-way line, eager to pick up anything that would allow him a chance to double his score (and he thought of the goals as his, not the Kings'). The tangerine-shirted players were still pressing forward and Alex was well aware that if he remained in his own half he couldn't be off-side whatever the number of players between him and the penalty area.

'Oh no!' screeched the Clocklane coach as, suddenly, one of his midfielders, lunging to pick up a loose ball, lost his footing and slid, flat on his back, so far that he crashed into a team-mate, bringing him down, too. The gap, as they both struggled to get to their feet, was huge. Foggy was the one to capitalize on it. Sprinting on to the ball, he then veered to his left to avoid the only opponent who was near him and still vertical. Alex, inevitably, called for the ball but Foggy ignored him; this was the moment for Marc Thrale, not Alex Todd, to enjoy the glory of a goal.

Only one outfield defender was in the Clocklane half of the pitch as Foggy powered on. They were, of course, on a collision course but Foggy was sure he had the beating of him; until, without noticing where he was heading, Foggy hit another boggy patch. His opponent loomed up, Foggy knew he was losing control of the ball and so when he heard the yell, 'Pass it, pass it!' he obeyed. He thought it must be the voice of Sam Saxton; instead, it was Ricky Todd's.

Alex, homing in on the ball like a bird returning to its favourite perch, took it at an angle into the corner of the box where, once again, the goalie had only his own instincts to save his team from further embarrassment. He came out at the crouch, arms spread as wide as possible to provide the biggest barrier as his coach was always telling him he should do.

It was all to no avail. Alex timed his strike beautifully, waiting until he was perfectly positioned to steer the ball wide of the advancing keeper and into the net near the base of the far post. No one could have scored with more aplomb.

Alex Todd 2, he exulted, Clocklane Strikers 0. Surely the game now belonged to Rodale Goal Kings. Unless someone else in the team did something really rash or stupid.

4 Pitch Invasion

While Ricky ecstatically applauded his son's achievement, and even the so far silent Karen clapped politely, Sam Saxton was intent on calming his team down. 'Settle, you've got to settle,' he called. 'Don't give it away now. Keep it tight!'

There was very little that was polite or thoughtful about the response from Clock-lane supporters. 'Get a grip, get a grip, Strikers!' was one demand while other voices lashed individual players for their laziness or stupidity. The rudest comments of all came from a woman who looked too young to be a player's mum. Perhaps, Ricky supposed, she was someone's sister; or possibly a player herself who was better than any Striker on the pitch.

The abuse and persistent orders to do this or that soon had an effect. As the Kings strove to add to their lead or contain the big Clock-lane forwards, tackles became ever fiercer, ankles were hacked, shirts yanked and, if the aggressors thought no official was watching, blows were struck. Because of his obvious scoring skills and potential Alex was a prime target. A clumsy lunge from behind when Alex next got possession earned a chunky Clocklane midfielder a stern finger-wagging and the second yellow card of the match. Alex made a great show of removing his shin pad and vigorously rubbing the affected area while sitting on the pitch.

'Should've been sent off for that!' Ricky told anyone who'd listen. 'Could cripple a player, charging him in the back like that.'

Yet, only minutes later, Alex went down again as a result of another full-blooded challenge from a full-back as the Kings' striker tried to outwit him with a clever flick-on to Lloyd Colmer. This time Alex, unscathed, jumped up and dived at his opponent. Both went down in a flurry of arms and legs until, fortunately, team-mates dragged them apart. Once again the ref issued dire warnings and then flourished the yellow card twice.

'You can't book Alex!' his father roared. 'He didn't start that. He's innocent!'

But the ref wasn't listening, even if anyone else was, and Alex's name had gone into his notebook. Alex, who'd taken a knock in the mouth and was wondering whether he was bleeding, for once had the good sense to say nothing. Reluctantly, he even shook hands with his attacker when the ref ordered them to make it up.

'Alex, son, go and get your hat-trick whatever else you do,' his father urged under his breath. 'That'll show this lot better than anything else anyone can do.'

For the moment, however, Alex was distinctly subdued and, in any case, play was taking place more in Rodale's half as Clocklane battled, in some cases literally, for a chance to reduce the deficit. Although the rain had eased into little more than a drizzle the playing surface was getting worse. Mud patches were bigger and deeper and few players were able to keep their footing for long except on the flanks. Dominic, who'd dropped back on receiving precise instructions from his coach, was keen to dribble his way out of trouble only to be ordered to 'hoof it away!' So he hoofed it. It wasn't something he enjoyed until he realized that at least he was giving his embattled fellow defenders some breathing space. So next time he had the ball he kicked it harder and higher than ever before and grinned when Sam applauded.

The Kings' coach was less pleased with some of Josh's work, however. When the tall, curly-haired midfielder slithered to a halt to keep his footing, thus allowing an opponent to take possession of the ball, Sam yelled, 'Should've got that, Josh, should've reached that!' Karen Rowley frowned and looked more worried than ever. What troubled her was that Josh was bound to be feeling the cold and that all this rain couldn't do him any good at all. Yet Josh himself wasn't betraying any anxiety about the weather; in truth, he hardly noticed the rain. All he could think about was playing well enough to retain his place in the Kings' line-up. Secretly, he still cherished hopes that one day he might take Alex's place as chief striker. Josh was convinced he'd score goals at an unbeatable rate.

In spite of all the furious endeavour, mis-kicks, skids and spectacular tumbles, skilful footwork and heroic tackling, no further goals were scored before half-time. As the players trooped off the pitch for oranges or energy bars or hot drinks thoughtfully provided for both teams by Clocklane supporters, Ricky Todd darted across for a word with his son.

'You're playing some wonderful stuff, Alex. You can't fail to be man-of-the-match,' he rejoiced. 'It was criminal the way you got a yellow card but don't let it upset you. This ref hasn't a clue. Doesn't know what he's seeing.'

That was truer than Mr Todd realized. The ref was an older man who'd only agreed to take this match to help out a friend who'd originally been allocated the game by the local football association but then needed a free day to visit his ailing mother. Although he didn't know it the ref was in the early stages of an attack of flu and still hadn't forced himself to take the eye-test he knew was necessary. So he wasn't seeing anything very clearly.

'I'm going to get that guy who got me,' Alex muttered, 'whatever I do. He's not getting away with nearly breaking my leg.' Once again he rolled down his sock to show his dad the extent of the bruising though not much was visible yet.

Ricky put his arm round the boy's shoulders. 'No attempts at retribution, Alex. Not worth it. Don't miss out on the hat-trick.'

That reminder calmed him. He wanted this third goal, wanted it more than anything else, but he was also incensed at the way the opposition were playing. They didn't seem to care what they kicked as long as it moved.

Ricky wasn't allowed in the dressing-room, of course, but he arrived at the door at the same moment as Sam. So he had to say what was in his mind. 'Another goal will kill off the opposition,' he pointed out. 'Nothing to be gained by just sitting on our lead.'

To his surprise the coach just nodded and there was even the hint of a smile. 'You could be right,' he admitted. Then he went inside, closing the door behind him.

'Enjoying it?' Ricky enquired, ranging alongside Karen Rowley.

'Hardly,' she muttered, turning to look at him with the sort of expression that suggested she couldn't believe anyone would ask such a stupid question.

He wasn't put off. 'Well, we're winning and the match is half over. Oh, and Josh seems to be having a decent game.'

She looked thoroughly surprised. 'D'you think so, really? Sam Saxton doesn't appear impressed. He's shouted at him at least twice.'

'Oh, that'll be par for the course,' Ricky tried to reassure her. All the same, he scented he had found another ally. 'Sam, er, sometimes has strange ideas about how to run the team.'

Mrs Rowley just nodded, her mind on something else. 'Does your Alex ever complain about the cold? You know, on a day like this. I can't believe Josh is really warm enough dressed like that. But he won't listen to me when he's in his passionate football mood.'

'I wouldn't worry if I were you. Boys of their age don't bother about the cold and wet unless they're standing still – or can use it as an excuse for playing badly! Today they seem to be overcoming the conditions better than Clocklane are.'

That comment proved untimely. The second half had barely begun when Clock-lane scored: but, unlike the Kings' early first goal, it wasn't from the penalty spot. Lloyd Colmer failed to control the ball on the edge of the centre circle and was horrified to see the boy who'd robbed him sprint away into a large open space. Josh, still nervous about his role in central defence, tried a tackle that was feeble in the extreme (so it was a good thing he couldn't see his coach's facial expression). For once even Joe Parbold was caught napping as the ball-runner whipped a splendid pass to Marcus. And Marcus, from just inside the box, surprised everyone by hitting the ball first time on the half-volley. Danny Loxham was just off his line and all he could do was watch the ball sail over his left shoulder into the net.

'Oh no!' Sam and Ricky chorused, although they were many metres apart and couldn't hear one another. Both felt the Kings didn't deserve to concede a goal after their heroic efforts in the first half to control the game. Sam knew he couldn't blame Danny but he couldn't resist a word to the real culprit.

'Get a grip, Josh!' he called, unwittingly echoing the words Clocklane supporters had used to their own team. 'Don't take your eye off the ball. Concentrate!'

Karen Rowley closed her eyes. She hadn't enjoyed much so far and now the game was turning into a nightmare. If Josh was as bad as the coach seemed to think then her son shouldn't be playing at all. It crossed her mind to have a word with Sam Saxton and ask him to replace Josh with someone else who might do a better job for him. After all, there were two boys just waiting to get on to the pitch. But she knew Josh would never forgive her if ever she did anything like that. She sighed. Boys needed to be tough to survive in this world her mother was always telling her. Karen supposed that was true but it wasn't easy to cope with that when the boy concerned was your only son who at this stage of his development was probably outgrowing his strength.

The goal had fired up the Strikers. What

they'd done once, they could do again. The equalizer was surely within their grasp. Their supporters, now more vocal then ever, bayed for blood. Marcus, as if sensing that the Rodale defence might be on the verge of panic, began to switch the direction of play with skill and imagination. His tallest teammate, Jacko, was proving adept at resisting any kind of tackle before firing the ball hard at Marcus to try another mazy run.

Believing that another goal must come, the Clocklane fans were constantly yelling, 'Go, Marcus, go!' Then, just as the orange shirts seemed to be everywhere in the Rodale box, Joe Parbold chested the ball down, evaded two tackles with rare footwork and then lofted the ball straight down the middle. Foggy, facing the ball as it came at him, moved to control it. But, not for the first time, he slipped. As his feet went from under him he somehow managed to lash out and performed an amazing scissors-kick that sent the ball flying up the pitch to where Alex was loitering with the intention of picking up anything that came his way. He was as happy to accept a freak chip as any precision pass and so he was on to it in a flash, eager to complete his hat-trick and the third goal that his dad had said at half-time would put the match beyond Clocklane's reach.

One defender had stayed back as if to keep his goalkeeper company as Alex decided that the arrow-straight path was the best route to goal. 'Yes, yes!' Ricky urged his son, for once keeping his voice down as if not wanting to put Alex off his stride. He was sure, sure beyond any shadow of doubt, that Alex would score. It was a situation just made for a proven goal-scorer of Alex's pace and skill: just one opponent to outwit and then a clear run towards a fairly helpless goalkeeper.

Alex, barely pausing to lean in one direction while swerving the other way to fool his nearer adversary, was already by-passing him when the stick-thin boy suddenly leapt sideways and sent Alex crashing to the ground. Completely unhurt because of the softness of the ground, Alex, fury in his heart, was just scrambling to his feet when the defender, also grounded, stretched out a long leg in an attempt to get the ball and managed only to send Alex tumbling again. Somehow, though, the Clocklane defender succeeded in keeping possession this time.

Alex was unable to control his anger. Without a split-second's thinking he stamped down on his opponent's thigh. It wasn't done to maim him and afterwards Alex would claim he was merely trying to wrest the ball free from an opponent who'd lost control of it.

The ref, however, saw things differently, though in truth he had witnessed hardly anything of the original skirmish because he was still too far from the play, having been stationed for some time on the edge of the opposite penalty area. The red card was in his hand, and being flourished high above his head, even before he reached the tangling pair.

'Vicious that was, downright vicious!' he thundered at Alex. 'Off you go, boy!'

'But I was – I was –' Alex tried to protest. But in vain. The ref would listen to no explanation because he didn't believe there was one.

'I've told you to go, so go,' he repeated. 'It will be worse for your team if you delay this game by so much as another second.'

Ricky, scarcely believing what he had seen, didn't waste a second either. Arm upraised to upbraid the official, he raced on to the pitch. He wasn't going to allow his and Alex's dreams to be destroyed by someone who hadn't a clue what he was doing.

Alex swallowed hard as he heard the ref's verdict. His instinct was to continue his protest in spite of all the warnings Sam had delivered about not getting into arguments with officials. Then, as he half turned away, he saw his father flying towards them, fist aloft. There was no doubt in Alex's mind what was going to happen if he didn't act swiftly.

He flung himself at his father, trying to pin his arms to his sides. 'Don't, Dad, don't!' he screamed in his ear. 'If you hit him they'll ban us both for ever. Then I'll never get another goal for anybody.'

That message went home. Ricky Todd shook his head at the horror of such an idea and allowed Alex to turn him about and usher him towards the touchline. As they walked off the pitch together it began to dawn on Ricky what a responsible attitude his son had taken.

'I'm proud of you, Alex, proud,' he told him fervently. 'It would have been so easy for you to have reacted as I did. I just wanted to flatten the guy for what he's done to you – and the Kings.'

'No, we'll still win,' said Alex confidently, though he didn't know whether he really believed that. 'That boy who tackled me – just like a bulldozer, he was – well, he ought to be sent off. He *deserves* that, I don't.'

Because they'd had their backs to the ref at the time they hadn't seen him bring out the yellow card as a result of the intervention by the assistant referee who'd gone over to describe his 'sideways shunt of a tackle' that triggered off the skirmish. The boy himself was still partly in tears as he rolled up his shorts to show the mark on his thigh caused by Alex's boot. In fact, it was little more than a muddy graze and the pain was barely noticeable. But the defender felt he needed to make the protest as strong as possible to impress his coach.

Sam Saxton was stalking towards his

dismissed striker. Plainly, he had something to say. 'Don't you listen to *anything* I tell you?' he demanded, glaring at Alex.

'What?' Alex replied. He hadn't a clue what the coach was getting at; and his mind was still in a whirl after the unfairness of the sending-off and his prompt action in preventing his dad from attacking the ref.

'*Be calm*, that's what I told you before this game. *Be calm*. That's the way to avoid trouble. But what d'you do? You get yourself sent off, that's what. Sent off because *calm* was the last thing you were. You were crashing around like a madman.'

'Hey, come off it, Sam! That's totally unfair,' Ricky protested. 'It's the other lad who was doing the madman impersonation. Didn't you *see* what he did to Alex, the way he brought him down? No wonder he retaliated. You'd've done the same if you'd been mugged like that.'

Sam shook his head. 'I certainly wouldn't. One of the first things I learned as a player was to control my temper. If you lose that you're in danger of losing everything else. I preach that to the Kings all the time. Of course, some boys have a memory problem.'

Ricky sounded as exasperated as he looked. 'Sam, nobody's perfect. If a boy's been badly treated by an opponent then it's natural for him to want to get his own back, to even things out.'

'Not when you know you can get yourself sent off for an offence like that,' Sam snapped back. 'Alex knew he had a yellow card, knew the ref was watching him. So, not for the first time, he acted without thinking, acted stupidly. I'm tempted to say I've also just seen where he gets his temper from.'

'OK, I know I was out of order running on to the pitch like that,' Ricky admitted to Sam's considerable surprise. 'But the way he's going on, that ref could lose the game for us. He hasn't a clue –'

'No, no, *you* could have lost it for us, Mr Todd!' Sam cut in, sensing the advantage was his at present. 'A pitch invasion by anyone can result in dire consequences for a team. We could be thrown out of the League if they felt you were representing Rodale Kings. Just as well you didn't lay a finger on the ref as I was sure you were going to.'

'He was only showing loyalty to Alex, to his son,' said Karen Rowley as the men paused before saying anything else. 'He wanted to defend him. That's what dads should do.'

Ricky shot her a grateful glance, not least because he was glad of the interruption. He didn't want to admit it but he knew Sam was right: he, Ricky Todd, really had made a serious error of judgement. Now he thought about it, he realized the Kings could be punished for his hasty action.

'Look, Sam –' he was starting to say when a sudden roar of excitement from the crowd made them all turn to the pitch.

After another midfield maul following Alex's dismissal and the yellow card shown to his opponent in their scuffle, the Strikers were launching another all-out attack. To no one's surprise, it was Marcus who got it under way with a very clever lob over Foggy's head to a team-mate patrolling the driest territory of all on the far wing. He, too, showed a deft touch when bringing the ball under control. 'Take it on, take it on!' his fans on the touchline yelled – and he did. Foggy, with his customary determination, gave chase but had no real hope of catching the fleet winger who, without warning, released the ball in a low centre to the corner of the penalty area.

Josh was the nearest player in a purple shirt and he simply didn't know how to deal with it when it came to him at waist height: it was too high for a kick and too low for a header. By the time he'd made his mind up to try with his head the ball had cannoned off his arm and the ref, rather too far away again from the action, whistled for a hand-ball offence. That was when the home fans erupted: a scoring chance would be there if only the free kick were productive. By now it was becoming clear that the Rodale team was nervous about the outcome of the match. Since losing their two-goal lead and their chief striker things seemed to have gone against them.

'Get back, Foggy!' Sam roared as the free kick was lined up against an under-strength defence. But Foggy's slowness in obeying meant there was one marker too few as the ball floated in from a well-driven kick.

Jacko, leaping the highest, got his forehead

to it and nodded it across towards Marcus. His aim, though, wasn't good and Dominic was perfectly placed to intercept. Woefully, he headed it so weakly that the ball merely dropped towards Clocklane's skipper. Marcus didn't miss a chance like that. With one thrust of his leg he steered the ball past Danny and into the net. And so the score was now 2–2.

'Kings, what are you thinking of?' Sam wailed. It was rare for him to display as much emotion as that in a crisis for he believed that if he displayed despair his team would catch the infection instantly. But it was a long time since he'd seen the Kings slump so quickly from a position of strength to one so weak they could be put out of the Cup in the next few moments.

Ricky Todd didn't say anything. He was as keen as everyone connected with the team to see them triumph at all times, to play so well that they were bound to collect a trophy. Yet he couldn't help feeling that defeat today would help his cause when people next decided who was best qualified to coach Rodale Goal Kings. 'Dad, we're going to lose this one if we give away another soft goal like that,' Alex pointed out. 'I mean, now I'm out of this game we've nobody up front to score for us.'

That was true, although once Sam had substituted another defender for Foggy and pushed Lloyd Colmer into an attacking role a goal chance was created out of almost nothing. Sent on his way by a long and accurate pass from Dominic, Lloyd accelerated impressively. With the Strikers' defence still out of place because of their own attacking instincts, Lloyd had plenty of room to work in and he easily rounded his one challenger. The sight of goal inspired him to try a snap shot. It was fierce and it was on target. But the goalie reached the ball, only to allow it to rebound from his chest. Lloyd, following up, slid in with both feet to try to turn it into the net, only to be foiled by the goalie's ability to stretch his fingers to the uttermost and flick the ball round the post for a corner kick.

All the Kings' tallest players descended on the goalmouth in the hope of forcing the ball into the net from what might be the last kick of the game. In unison they jumped, and in unison they all missed the ball as it came over.

The goalkeeper, redeeming himself for his earlier lapse, managed to soar high enough to grab the ball and this time hug it safely to his chest. And just as Joe Parbold had guessed when he trotted upfield for that corner, the ref immediately blew for full-time.

So it was to be a penalty shoot-out, the first the Kings had ever experienced.

'Oh no!' Alex suddenly exclaimed. 'They won't let me take a penalty because I've been sent off. Disaster! I'd've scored for sure.'

Sam at that moment was thinking exactly the same thing. Before setting out for the game he'd worked out his shooting order if it came down to penalties and Alex would've taken the first. Now he had to choose someone else for perhaps the most important kick in Rodale's brief history. For if it were missed then the opposition would secure a huge psychological advantage. In his mind it was a toss-up between Joe and Danny, and the mental coin came down in Joe's favour.

Clocklane had won the toss and their coach decided they'd shoot first. Marcus confidently stepped up, put the ball on the spot, turned, turned again, ran up – and missed!

Most of his fans were open-mouthed as the ball skidded well wide of the left-hand post. Marcus himself sank to his knees, his head in his hands. He knew the treacherous surface had spoilt his aim but it was still almost impossible for him to believe the ball wasn't in the back of the net. As gently as possible, the ref assisted Marcus to his feet so that Joe could take the first kick for Rodale.

And Joe, too, fired wide. He couldn't blame the surface because he struck the ball well enough for it to be still rising as it zipped past the right-hand post. So, suddenly, the Clocklane fans could smile again, however briefly. Less attractively, a couple of their more vocal female supporters cheered loudly. To his credit, the ref called out; 'We don't want any of that, thank you. If you're a true supporter of football you don't cheer a boy's unhappiness.'

It was just as well he said that because the next shooter, Jacko, also failed to hit the target, the ball sailing high over the bar; and Jacko stumbled away, his face also hidden in his hands.

'Don't believe it!' Ricky gasped. 'Can't

anyone put the ball in the net? It's big enough – the net I mean.'

Because he guarded one all the time, Danny knew exactly how huge the space seemed to any goalkeeper facing an opponent with the ball at his feet. Now that it was his turn to shoot he knew what he would do. He aimed for the top of the net to the left of the keeper and, unhurriedly and positively, he drove the ball into that gap. The net bulged and the Rodale contingent, players and fans alike, cheered furiously to register their relief.

'Go on, miss, miss, miss!' Alex urged under his breath as a Clocklane defender went up to take the next kick. With all his being he wanted Rodale to win this game so that he could go on to score a hat-trick in another round and eventually pick up the medal he was convinced he deserved.

Alex got his wish. In his anxiety to do the right thing the kicker failed to get the direction right even though he hit the ball well enough. It flew, chest-height, straight at Danny and Danny gratefully cradled it to his midriff.

'Incredible! Three misses on the trot!' a

furious Clocklane supporter yelled to the heavens. 'You're rubbish, you lot. Strikers? You couldn't strike a single note on a piano!'

Nobody laughed, not even a Rodale fan. But then, moments later all Rodale had plenty to celebrate as Lloyd Colmer, to his intense delight, whacked the ball home well beyond the goalkeeper's despairing dive. Rodale 2, Clocklane 0 – with two penalties to each side still remaining.

The next cheer was all too obviously ironic. For a Clocklane midfielder became the first player on his side to find the net, thumping his shot over Danny's flailing arms into the roof of the net. He raised his own arms high above his head to register his pleasure but none of his team-mates rushed across to congratulate him. By now they all believed the Cup-tie was as good as lost. Only a kind of miracle could save them. None, so far, had any reason to believe in miracles.

The Rodale players knew that so long as they scored from either of the next two attempts they were through to the next round. Josh Rowley could hardly wait to get there. Before anyone else could get to the ball he seized it, planted it on the spot, waited a moment for the ref's signal – and then banged it as hard as he could. His desperate wish to score a goal for the Kings could so easily have been achieved in that moment. Instead, by the margin of a few millimetres, he failed.

The ball struck the base of the upright and rebounded to Josh who promptly hit it into the net. Of course, it didn't count. Josh was just as distraught as the other four players who'd failed from the spot. Not only had he missed a vital goal, he'd almost certainly have to face the wrath of Sam Saxton for taking a kick he hadn't been nominated for; and so, probably, he'd never be picked for the team again. He slunk away, unable to look anyone in the eye. Karen Rowley wished with all her heart that she dare rush on to the pitch and put her arms round him; but she knew that was the last thing he'd want. Josh would never live it down with his team-mates.

Hope was rising again for Clocklane: they hadn't lost yet. Nearly – but not quite. And that hope suddenly ascended steeply as the Strikers' centre back very calmly hoofed the ball into the right-hand side of the net as

Danny leapt after it just a fraction too late. Clocklane 2, Rodale 2 – with just one kick left of the obligatory five-per-side. If the Kings scored, they'd win; if they failed then it would be sudden death with victory going to the first side to score when their opponents missed.

'Go on, Dominic, you can do it – I know you can!' Alex called, although no one had noticed he had his fingers crossed. Many of the spectators simply couldn't look at the scene in the goalmouth as Dominic Allenby slowly placed the ball on the spot after deliberately cleaning the mud off it with his shirt. No one could have guessed from his manner how nervous he felt. 'Good luck, son, just take your time,' Sam murmured, though his words went unheard.

The goalkeeper, arms spread wide as he crouched on his line, watched hawk-like as Dominic stepped back several paces. Then, in almost complete silence all around the pitch, Dominic ran in, checked suddenly, and then drove an angled shot as cleanly as any-one could wish into the net just inside the right-hand upright.

'Yes!' the Rodale fans exulted, many of them dashing across to congratulate the scorer in hugs of delight. But, of course, his team-mates got there first and Dominic disappeared beneath a steepling pile of purple shirts.

'You'd think we'd won the Cup, not just the first round game,' murmured Karen Rowley as Ricky vigorously joined in the applause, his hands high above his head. Alex was somewhere in the midst of the continuing joyfulness on the pitch where Sam Saxton was trying to get a sensible word with each of his players in turn.

'Well, it must feel like that to them, I suppose,' Ricky pointed out. 'Let's face it, they were within one kick of defeat, weren't they?'

Only when he saw the expression on Karen's face did he realize how foolish his comment was. 'Oh, er –' he started to say.

'I know, I know,' she interrupted wanly. 'Honestly, I don't know how Josh is going to get over that miss. I know how desperately he wants to score a goal for the Kings. This football just seems to take over his life, you know. I just wish he could be a, well, a bit more relaxed about it.'

'Oh, they're pretty resilient, most kids,' Ricky grinned, hoping to give some comfort. 'I mean, Alex's just the same. His world ends one minute when something goes wrong in a match, like being subbed when he was on a hat-trick; but the next minute, well, by the next match, anyway, he's on a high again. That's kids, isn't it? Just as well, too!'

'Hope you're right,' said Karen, looking as sad as she sounded. 'But you see, I have the impression that the coach isn't going to forgive Josh for that miss. He was very critical of him long before that – throughout the game, really. Always finding faults. You must have heard him.'

Ricky nodded. 'I did. But, you know, Sam has a bit of a thing about the defence, it's his only focus really. So if anyone makes even the tiniest slip-up he's on to it like lightning.' He paused and glanced across at the last of the players to leave the pitch and, on the opposite touchline, some of the still inconsolable Clocklane families. 'But he nearly slipped up himself this time, did our Sam. I mean, he worries so much about defending he sometimes forgets he's got a good attack. He ought to have been encouraging the Kings to go all-out for goals from the moment we got the first two. Then this lottery of the shoot-out would never have been necessary. I hope he's going to look at things differently next time.'

'If there is a next time – for Josh, I mean,' Karen said.

Ricky Todd didn't find it hard to share her worries. 'Well, we're all in the same boat there, Karen. Never know what our coach is going to do next, do we?'

5 The Boy from Bordeaux

Karl-Heinz Bruggemann wasn't quite what Kieren Kelly had expected. Perhaps because of old films he'd seen on TV he imagined that most Germans were tall and blond with sharp features. Karl-Heinz was dark and stocky and round-faced. He didn't say much about anything so you couldn't tell what he was thinking. And why, Kieren asked himself, did he have to have two first names? Wasn't one good enough for him?

He would have liked to ask those questions of the boy himself but Kieren's mother was adamant that he should be extremely careful in everything he said. 'Don't forget, Karl-Heinz has had a very difficult time lately, to put it mildly. His parents have split up and his dad's working like mad to get his new restaurant in Bordeaux open on time. So he's bound to feel pretty lonely, even miserable, at times. We've got to do our very best to make him feel completely at home. And one other thing: don't go on about football. In fact, try not to mention it at all if he doesn't. Not everybody's mad about the game like you. Very likely he plays tennis – Germans are good at that, aren't they? I mean, their players keep winning at Wimbledon. Or maybe he goes swimming, or prefers chess or something like that. So play it very carefully, Kieren, all right?'

Kieren still didn't know why the German was staying with them in the first place. His mum merely explained that Karl-Heinz's dad was an old friend and she'd offered to help him out at a particularly difficult time for Herr Bruggemann. Already she'd had several late night telephone conversations with him, presumably about how Karl-Heinz was settling in. Because he couldn't sleep one night and had gone downstairs for a fizzy drink, Kieren had heard his mum talking on the phone and some of the conversation was in German, a language she nonchalantly said she'd 'picked up when I was young – in my teens, actually.'

He was sticking to his promise to say nothing about football. But then he was sure Karl-Heinz wasn't interested in the game anyway. He was the wrong sort of shape for a player, in Kieren's experience, and when some soccer highlights were about to be shown on a TV programme Karl-Heinz just shrugged in reply to Kieren's question about watching it. So, to be polite, Kieren switched the set off. It wasn't as if he couldn't understand the language. His English appeared to be just as good as his French. For his part, Kieren knew scarcely a word of German.

Now he had the problem of finding something for them to do that evening that Karl-Heinz might enjoy. He didn't seem to like board games and the only things that interested him on TV were programmes about France and cooking: a programme about French cuisine would be perfect but there was nothing at all like that on any channel that evening. Then, to Kieren's delight, Dominic rang up with the excellent suggestion that they should go and collect some wood for Bonfire Night and try to raise money for the Guy at the same time. When Kieren mentioned Karl-Heinz, Dominic's response was immediate: 'Bring him along. Give him a chance to see an ancient British custom. Bet they haven't anything like Bonfire Night where he comes from.'

Karl-Heinz was frankly amazed by what Kieren told him. 'You mean they put this guy on top of a fire-pile and burn him to death? That is, how d'you say, *barbaric*. Nobody would treat a criminal like that in my country.'

'Oh yes they would,' Dominic cut in sharply. 'Don't you know about Joan of Arc? The French burnt her at the stake. Just the same thing. And she wasn't doing anything as bad as trying to blow up the government.'

That provoked only a shrug. 'That is the French. Remember I am German. The French, too, are barbaric sometimes. I really admire only their cooking. My father also says the best thing about France is the food.'

'Look, it's only a bit of fun, this Guy Fawkes stuff,' Kieren broke in, fearing that if the talk went on in this way there'd soon be an international flare-up in Rodale Kings. 'We don't have to get involved tonight if you don't want to. I mean, we could do something else. Don't know what, though.'

'If we collect just a bit of cash we could get something to eat,' Dominic suggested. 'My folks are both out so I didn't get much for tea tonight. Fact is, I'm starving! Quite fancy some fish and chips. How about you, Karl-Heinz? Bet they don't have them in France, do they?'

The sensitive German nose wrinkled. 'I think not. In a real restaurant, definitely not. I do not care for such food, thank you.'

'Karl-Heinz really just likes pancakes. He makes loads and loads of them all the time,' said Kieren. 'They're good too. Can't eat as many as he does, though.'

'But don't you eat them with syrup and sugar and sweet stuff like that?' Dominic asked.

'Oh yes, of course,' agreed Karl-Heinz, his eyes brightening.

'Well, that's not for me,' said Dominic, glancing at Karl-Heinz's less than trim out-line. 'I prefer the savoury stuff, that terrific tang of the vinegar on the fish and the chips.' By now, though, he realized he wasn't going to enjoy that taste tonight, at least not if he remained with these two. Trouble was, Kieren worried too much about almost everything and Dominic guessed that his team-mate had to go along with whatever Karl-Heinz wanted. Probably that was what Mrs Kelly had told him to do.

'So, what'd you like to do, Karl-Heinz?' Dominic asked as cheerfully as possible.

'I cannot say, I do not know what choices there are,' was the unexpectedly frank reply. 'Do you have something you like to do? Except eat these chips-with-fish, I mean?'

'I was thinking of going over to the leisure centre. There's some five-a-side football training and – and . . .' Dominic broke off as he saw Kieren's eyes open wide, followed by some desperate head-shaking. Obviously, there was something he shouldn't mention.

'Football?' Karl-Heinz said, his eyes widening, too, but apparently in eager anticipation rather than despair. 'You have football here in this village? Then I –'

'Look, hang on,' Kieren chimed in. 'You see, I'm not supposed to mention football at all when Karl-Heinz is around. Mum –'

Now the German boy looked bewildered. 'Not *mention* it? But why not? What is wrong with the football, please?'

Kieren gulped. 'It's Mum, actually. She says I'm obsessed with football, you know, mad about the game. Never think of anything else. Well, she thought I shouldn't say anything about it to you in case you're not interested in football. So if you don't like it, well, you wouldn't have to show an interest just to be polite. See what I mean?'

Karl-Heinz suddenly laughed, something that hadn't happened often since his arrival in Rodale as the guest of the Kelly family. 'Not *interested*? That is funny. I am – how do you say it? – mad about football, too. At home I play the football all the time. That is my home in Germany. In France I play, too. Not as much as we only just now moved there.'

'But you didn't say anything about that when those football highlights came up on TV,' Kieren pointed out. 'You turned your head away and I turned the set off.'

'Ja. That is so. My father, he says I am not to speak of it in England if possible. He thinks the English are not good at football. He –'

'What! But we beat Germany to win the World Cup Final!' Dominic almost screeched in his excitement to point out that fact.

'Ja. I know that. My father knows really nothing about the football. That is why he says nothing when I play so much. Also, he is very, very busy making his new restaurant.'

'You'd like to play here, then, wouldn't you?' Dominic asked eagerly.

'Of course! I like to play the football all the time wherever I go. It is the most important thing in the world for me.' He turned a sly grin on Kieren. 'Ja, even better than the pancakes!'

'So what're we waiting for?' Dominic cried. 'Let's get off to the leisure centre.'

They moved with the speed of a top striker scenting an opening in a crowded goalmouth. Kieren didn't know about the five-a-side training session but he wasn't surprised that Dominic did; Dominic was increasingly ambitious and pushy and seemed to be improving his game all the time. Perhaps, Kieren reflected, Dominic had secret practice matches at the leisure centre quite regularly. If so, Kieren vowed, he'd ask to join in so that he improved his chances of turning out for the Kings in every match. Now, his excitement rose at the prospect of doing some training with players he might not even have met before. And what about Karl-Heinz? Would he be any good? Even if he was hopeless that hardly mattered because at least they could now talk openly about their favourite game at home.

Karl-Heinz wasn't hopeless at all. He was brilliant. That was the only word for his ball skills as Kieren mentally acknowledged after watching him for less than a couple of minutes. Despite the fact that he had to play in ordinary trousers and shoes because none of them had any kit with them Karl-Heinz performed as if the ball were attached to his feet by an invisible cord whenever he took an opponent on in a dribble or twisted and spun away to keep possession while being challenged by defenders. He could shoot powerfully with either foot and those shots scarcely ever rose above ankle-height.

For some reason nobody could explain only a handful of players had turned up for the training so when the three of them rushed in they were warmly welcomed. Pippa Jardine, wife of a local referee, was in charge so it didn't surprise Kieren that two of the players were girls.

They could play well, too, and Anya, particularly noticeable for the length of her dark hair, was quite ferocious when tackling anyone. Mrs Jardine, who had ambitions to become a League referee herself, allowed no fouls or deliberate mistakes to go unpunished.

Lloyd Colmer was the only other Goal King present and he greeted his team-mates with a dazzling display of dribbling until Hayley accidentally or on purpose bumped into him. Lloyd went tumbling but got no sympathy when he complained he'd bruised his knee. Even Mrs Jardine turned a blind eye to the offence for once.

'That's Lloyd's trouble, gives the ball away too easily,' Kieren confided to Karl-Heinz. 'That's what Sam Saxton said when I was on the bench – er, substitute, I mean.'

'They don't get me off so easily,' Karl-Heinz declared. 'The ball and I, we are like two feet. We are always together. One is no good without the other, ja?'

'Yes,' Dominic agreed.

'Glad that girl's not in any of the teams the Kings play,' remarked Lloyd as he came across to join them during the interval when they could have a drink if they wished. 'Like a castle door, she is. You've no hope of getting past her if she wants to close you down.'

'Well, she'd be no bother to Karl-Heinz here,' Kieren observed. 'The way he plays, he'd get around any opposition, no danger. Wish he played for the Kings. Then we'd easily be the best in the League.'

'I also wish that,' the German boy said quietly.

For a moment or two no one else said anything. It was Dominic who reacted first. 'Well, why not?' he wondered aloud. 'Why can't you play for us?'

Danny Loxham zoomed up the makeshift ramp, twisted in mid-air and then landed with perfect balance on the all-weather surface of the tennis court.

'Yes!' he exulted. 'Yes! That's the way to do it. Go on, then, Josh, try and beat that. Bet you can't.'

Josh Rowley knew he had no hope of getting anywhere near Danny's achievement and not for the first time wished he hadn't agreed to join in this impromptu skateboarding exhibition under the floodlights of Court Gardens Tennis Club where, earlier, Danny had been playing a couple of sets against Foggy Thrale. Josh had only dropped in to have a word with the Kings' goalkeeper about something rather personal. But Danny's enthusiasm for involving everyone in whatever he was doing himself was difficult to resist. In any case, Josh really needed his help.

Just coming down the slope in the middle of the rockery was hard enough. Twice he lost his balance and had to step off the virtually uncontrollable contraption. So there was no hope of building up enough momentum to attack the ramp at the necessary speed.

'Sorry,' he said abjectly, handing the board back to Danny. 'Just not my thing I'm afraid.'

'You're *hopeless* at it, that's what you are!' guffawed Foggy. 'Just like you are at soccer. I'd give up games now if I were you, Josh, I really would.'

'Hey, come on, Fog, that's not fair,' Danny protested. 'I know Josh didn't have a good game against Clocklane but, well, not many of us did. You weren't so great yourself. Sam –'

'Didn't miss a penalty, though, did I?' Foggy shot back. 'Didn't nearly lose the shoot-out for us!'

'Foggy, that's totally out of order!' Danny shouted. 'You never had a chance of taking a penalty because you'd already been substituted. You were having such a bad time Sam took you off.'

'No, no, that's rubbish. He was just giving me a breather before our next game against Scarinish. He'd knew I'd worked my socks off running all over the pitch on Sunday so I'd earned a break,' Foggy crowed. 'Not like you, Josh. You did nothing right. Sam'll give you a permanent rest, I reckon.'

'Keep your voice down, Fog!' Danny ordered, oblivious to the fact that he himself had been talking loudly. He was beginning to be embarrassed on Josh's behalf but he couldn't think of anything else to say. 'Anybody could be listening. Oh, and we're not supposed to be skateboarding, anyway.'

'My voice is my trademark, that's what everybody says,' boasted Marc Thrale as he built up speed down the rockery slope. In his opinion most spectators these days felt free to speak their mind and make all manner of criticism of players. So he didn't see why he shouldn't say what he felt, too. It was his view that Josh Rowley was a liability to the Kings and there was no way his deficiencies could be concealed on the pitch.

Danny shook his head in disappointment at Foggy's unnecessary outspokenness. Remarks like that could easily undermine team spirit. He, too, was aware of Josh's limitations but at the same time he appreciated the curly-haired full-back's determination to do his best for the team. It had also taken courage to volunteer for that crucial penalty kick: and, after all, he'd missed only by the narrowest margin.

'Josh, you said you wanted a word about something,' Danny put in quietly as Foggy gathered speed as he targeted the ramp. 'D'you want to say it now?'

'Er, no, not really, Danny,' mumbled Josh,

the pink glow on his cheeks only just starting to fade. 'It's nothing important. Look, I've got to go now, got to do some tidying up at home. See you.'

'See you,' Danny agreed, wondering what was really bothering Josh. Oh well, perhaps it was nothing of importance.

Josh forced himself to walk normally and not to run. But he felt he needed to get away as fast as possible. It simply hadn't been the right moment to try to enlist the help of Danny, Sam's favourite player, in keeping his place in the team. If anyone could persuade Sam to a certain course of action it surely must be the talented goalkeeper. But maybe, Josh decided gloomily, it would never be the right time to ask for Danny's help. If Danny was as honest as he appeared then he probably believed, just like Foggy, that Josh wasn't good enough for the Kings. So he wouldn't be prepared to plead for him with the coach.

'So what d'you think Kirsty really meant by that remark just when her boyfriend left?' Marina Saxton asked her husband as she used the remote control to extinguish the TV soap they never missed.

'What?' asked Sam vaguely. 'What was that?'

She sighed her well-practised sigh. 'You weren't listening to a word, were you, either their words or mine? Can't you just relax for once and *share* a bit of drama with me now and again? Not much to ask, Sam, not really.'

He'd picked up on one thing. 'Plenty of real drama out there, I reckon. Brewing up. I can feel it in my blood whenever these parents get together. Or simply when Ricky Todd is around and –'

'Oh, for heaven's sake, not the Kings again! Can't you switch off for just one evening? I mean, if you packed 'em up tomorrow life would still go on for them, they'd find someone else and –'

'No, no, you're the one not listening, my love!' he cut back. 'I'm not worried about the *team*, it's the families that bother me. The ones who are getting more and more involved and are going to cause trouble all round, I'll bet. Always happens when parents think they know more about football than the coach. I'll tell you what, the coach, *this* coach, anyway, me, I know more about their kids than they do themselves. And I'm not just talking about their skills on the pitch. Their characters, the real *them*, the brains behind the eyes, that's what I mean.'

She had been going to get up to make some coffee but stayed where she was for the time being. She hadn't heard Sam quite so worked up as this for a long time. 'What's brought this on? You won on Sunday, didn't you? I gathered it was touch and go at one point but, well, the Kings are in the next round. So . . .'

'Victory isn't everything, and I don't usually say that, do I? It's a lack of discipline I worry about. Well, I do after Ricky Todd's exhibition against Clocklane.'

'But he merely ran on to the pitch, didn't he, from what one of the mums told me at the baker's?'

'That was the trouble: because nothing happened he got away with it. He'll feel he can do anything he likes from now on. He's already rounding up some of the parents to get them to see things his way. I'm convinced of that, Rina.'

She sighed again. 'Conspiracies, conspiracies! You're forever suspecting them, Sam. I remember when you coached Hamrun Colts. You convinced yourself that newsagent – what was his name? Oh yes, Kennaway – well, that he was organizing a takeover, just because he wanted to sponsor all their kit. He was just a *supporter*, Sam, wanted a bit of advertising space, that was all. You had to admit it later.'

'I did,' he conceded, 'but this is different. Things have got much less friendly these last couple of seasons. Parents used to just watch and clap politely when their boys did something skilful or the team scored. Now they seem to want to control things, almost everything. Just like they've got a big say in how schools are run these days. Parent governors and those sort of people have power nowadays. It's getting that way in soccer. If it goes on like this, Rina, I'll be giving up, and soon. They can run their own teams in their own way if that's what they want. I'll clear out.'

She leaned across and kissed him. 'No you won't, Sam. You've said this sort of thing umpteen times but you don't do it. You've built the Kings up and you've said yourself they're getting better and better. You can't abandon them now if they're on the threshold of real success.'

Sam shrugged. 'Well, I can, you know. If Ricky Todd gets up to any more of his tricks and puts us at risk then I'll walk away. I really will. I may have said this before but this time I mean it.'

'Sam, I think you could be exaggerating all this. Ricky must really care about the Kings to do what he did, just as he cares about Alex. They want success for the team as well as for themselves.'

'That's the problem,' responded Sam, rising to his feet to put an end to the conversation. 'He cares all right – cares too much and in the wrong way.'

'Hi, Karen, how're you?' Ricky Todd greeted her cheerfully when Mrs Rowley opened her front door in answer to his ring. 'Hope I'm not interrupting anything. Not having a meal, are you?'

'No, we finished eating hours ago. You always eat early when you've got children, don't you?' she said, wondering what on earth he wanted. 'You're not here to sell me one of your sofas, I imagine. Anyway, come in.'

'No, nothing like that. I let the salesmen pick up their own commissions,' he laughed, following her into the sitting-room where Lloyd's mother, Serena Colmer, was sitting in an easy chair, sipping an interesting-looking drink. 'Oh, sorry. Wouldn't have dropped in on you like this, Karen, if I'd known you'd already got a visitor. I'll, er –'

'Ricky, sit down, do, you're not inter-rupting anything,' Karen invited brightly. 'In fact, if you've come about football you've timed your visit quite well. We're just talking about the team. Or maybe you *have* come about something else?'

'Definitely not! Actually, I was just wonder-ing how things are with Josh. I mean, he must be feeling a bit sick at being dropped for the next match. Especially coming on top of his penalty miss against Clocklane. I know ex-actly how Alex would feel – gutted. That's their word, isn't it?'

'You can say that again, twice over – double

gutted,' she agreed. 'Never seen him so low. I'm just thankful he's found something to do this evening instead of moping around the house all the time. That's what it's been like ever since he got the news. He and Danny are doing a bit of training together. At least, that was the idea.'

'Lloyd's not feeling a whole lot better, come to that,' Mrs Colmer put in while Karen got a drink for Ricky. 'He might be one of the subs or he might not, the coach isn't saying for certain. Lloyd thinks he's being punished for not doing too well last Sunday. But he's so keen, you know, keener than a sharp knife. He'd run through a wall for that team. But it won't last, this keenness, if he gets badly treated. That is what I want to tell the coach but Lloyd doesn't want me to say a word. Thinks it'll make more difficulties for him.'

'That's why Serena dropped in, to see what I thought,' said Karen. Her laugh was an attempt at light-heartedness but there was a hollow ring to it. 'You know, I thought the Kings were supposed to be doing well and yet look at us, all we've got is problems with our sons. Well, not you, Ricky, but –'

'Oh yes, definitely me as well,' Ricky put in quickly, glad to seize his opportunity to say what he'd come to say. 'Alex is also having a bad time with Sam. Just as with your boys, he doesn't know how to treat him. Sam really hasn't a clue about forward play, doesn't know what makes strikers tick, how they react to refs and encouragement. That's what they all need. And they're not getting it.'

There could be no doubt he had their support. Both women were nodding vigorously.

'You see, Sam only really cares about his defence. If the defence is right, the team can't go wrong. That seems to be his motto. But attacks win matches at this level, not defences. I mean, we were two up on Sunday and cruising. Another goal would have clinched it but what does Sam do: concentrates on defence, that's what he does. Then when players don't fit in with his plans for any reason he wants to punish 'em. Drops them from the side completely or leaves them on tenterhooks.'

'That's exactly what it is, punishment!'

Serena declared. 'And another thing: it's undermining Lloyd's confidence. Like I said, if he's wanted he'll run through fire. But the way it is now he's beginning to wonder whether he's any good at all. I know him, Ricky, I know what's going on in his head.'

Ricky nodded. 'Of course. That's why we care so much as parents, because we understand their needs. We want the best for them, not hassle and uncertainty. So we've got to do something about this situation before it's too late. I think –'

'I'll tell you how I feel,' interrupted Karen, anxious not to be left out of the conversation in her own home. 'I feel so strongly I'd be willing to buy new kit for the entire team, entire squad if you like, if that would guarantee a permanent place in the side for Josh. I mean it.'

Neither of her listeners doubted her. Serena wished she could make a similar offer, except that, as a single parent, she couldn't afford such a gesture. With Ricky that unexpected offer triggered off a new thought, something that probably would never have occurred to him under other circumstances.

'That's generous, Karen, very generous,' Ricky said approvingly. 'It's something we should bear in mind for the future. It demonstrates the depth of support we parents are prepared to give to the team to make sure *everyone* is involved as they deserve to be. Listen, d'you know any others who might want to join with us to get things changed?'

They discussed a number of names but couldn't come up with anyone who, they guessed, might feel as strongly as they did. Ricky, eager to collect all the support possible, mentioned those he could think of but the women shook their heads.

'Possibly Jane Allenby, I suppose,' said Serena when it seemed the list might be exhausted. 'Don't see much of her because her job is so, well, unpredictable, isn't it? Who knows when a midwife's going to be sure of time for herself? But Dominic's keen, just like Lloyd, and he's sometimes in the side, sometimes not. I know his dad doesn't have much interest in soccer. So maybe Jane would be willing to go along with us.'

Ricky said enthusiastically: 'Good, good. I'll try to see her, though if either of you get hold of her first do say I'd like a word. We've got to take action pretty soon before things get worse. I know we won on Sunday but if we play like that again we'll be losers.'

They nodded and he assumed he had their complete agreement. He was about to get to his feet when Karen asked the question he'd been half hoping for, half dreading. 'Ricky, suppose it was decided the Kings ought to dump Sam Saxton for one reason or another. Who would we get to take over? We've got to have someone the boys trust. Oh, and of course, someone who'd be a better coach and take the team forward. No point in changing just for the sake of it and getting no improvement.'

'I agree wholeheartedly,' he said with a broad, and he hoped winning, smile. 'Well, if you don't think I'm being big-headed in saying this, I think I've got the qualifications and I've certainly got the commitment. You know how much the team means to me, Karen. Only the other week when I was at the training session I took over some of the work from Sam – with his complete approval, I must add. The boys responded really well.

In fact, a couple of them said they'd enjoyed it better than any training they'd done for ages.'

He could sense from their expressions that they might not yet be convinced of his suitability for the role. His smile widened as he continued; 'Also, I have played the game myself, you know. Was quite a useful striker for Bovington United in my, er, well younger days. Though not as long ago as you might think! Also, I'm willing to put in the time required. My business is going pretty well so I can spare extra time if it's needed. Oh yes, one other thing: I know you've seen how good Alex is both on the ball and scoring goals. Well, maybe a dad shouldn't be saying this so bluntly, but he has learned a lot from me personally. We've done a lot of ball work together.'

Karen nodded but her smile wasn't as warm as he'd've liked. 'Ricky, I'm sure all that's true. I'm sure you have excellent credentials for coaching the Kings. But I think there is one area where there could be a problem: Alex. I mean, you can hardly be unbiased about the formation of the team when your own son is one of the players, can you? Also, what the other boys say and do when they're all together will get back to you. Bound to. Alex will be a sort of spy, won't he, even if he doesn't mean to be? It's just the way children are with each other. Don't you agree, Serena?'

And Serena nodded at once. 'Yes, I can see little difficulties ahead,' she said, though she smiled as she spoke as if unsure how serious the subject was.

'Honestly, I'm sure there won't be a problem,' Ricky said in his most positive tone. 'I can be objective when I need to be. You quickly learn that when you're running your own business with lots of employees to consider. Listen, there've been really top managers who have had a son playing for their first team. I remember years ago Brian Clough at Nottingham Forest played his son Nigel in the first team all the time; and Nigel didn't do so badly because he also played for England. The other players simply accepted the situation. And that's only one instance. Happens in junior football all the time, believe me.'

His explanation sounded convincing to him and he thought they were convinced, too. So he went on: 'If Alex *does* bring home tales of what other players are saying and doing, well, I'll be bound to listen. But I promise you this: I'll always listen to every other player as well and treat them with the same kind of honesty. Remember this: if you don't like what I'm doing, or the team starts to go downhill, well, you can always sack me! Or if you don't, I'll resign and *insist* someone else takes over. Is that fair?'

They could hardly deny it. Basically, they liked Ricky Todd and recognized that he had the team's interests at heart. He wouldn't have been talking to them like this if he didn't care deeply about the Goal Kings. So they must be prepared to trust his judgement in playing matters.

'Good,' he enthused as they nodded their acceptance. 'Right, anything else you can think of that we ought to talk about?'

'No,' they agreed after a suitable pause for thought. 'You seem to have covered everything.'

After thanking them for their support and

promising he'd be in touch again as soon as possible he suddenly paused on the doorstep, having remembered one name he ought to have mentioned. 'Oh yes, what about Jakki Kelly? Kieren's always on the fringes of the team, isn't he? I'm sure he wants more involvement.'

'Oh, I don't think you'll be lucky there,' Serena supposed. 'Jakki is wanting to calm things down as far as football is concerned.'

'Really?' his eyebrows shot up in disbelief.

'Well, yes, because of this foreign visitor, you see,' Serena tried to explain. 'He probably hates football and she doesn't want Kieren to upset him in any way. So she's told Kieren to give the game a rest for the time being, at least until this visitor has returned home. So, Ricky, I reckon you'd be wasting your time trying to get Jakki's support.'

6 'What a Goal!'

'So, who's that then?' one of the occasional supporters asked Melanie Todd as the Rodale Goal Kings trotted out on to the pitch for the home League match against Scarinish Town Boys. 'Never seen him before. And, I must say, he looks a trifle overweight to me for football.'

'Maybe that's because he likes extra helpings of trifle whenever it's on the menu!' Melanie laughed. 'Sorry, just a little joke. Actually, it may not be far from the truth because his dad is a chef. Runs his own restaurant in France, though he's German. Anyway, that's Karl-Heinz in the number eight shirt. He's playing up front with Alex, so Alex is naturally hoping he's as good as some of the other kids say he is.'

'Oh,' said the occasional supporter, having heard a great deal more than she'd expected to or even wanted to hear. After all, she was present only as a favour to her sister whose son was playing in the game. Personally, she found football a bore.

There was nothing boring about the start of the match, however, for it even gripped the attention of the irregular spectator. Scarinish began like a whirlwind. Within seconds their blue and black striped shirts seemed to be all over the Kings' penalty area and the fans they'd brought with them made encouraging noises out of all proportion to their numbers. Scarinish wasn't really big enough to be a town, anyway, but the football club lacked nothing in ambition. They believed they could win every game they played by a cricket score and thus, rather like Clocklane, Kings' previous opponents, they went in for instant and all-out attacks. In fact, they were just the sort of team that Ricky Todd admired and wanted the Kings to emulate.

Kieren Kelly was the first home defender to buckle under the prolonged assault by the Boys. He was in the side not only because his family had introduced Karl-Heinz to the team but mainly because someone had to take Josh Rowley's place, Josh having been dropped as a result of his poor performance against Clocklane. Kieren, surprised and delighted to be chosen, was determined to put on the sort of display that would ensure Sam Saxton wouldn't drop him in future. Sadly, Sam was regretting picking him within a couple of minutes of the kick-off. For when the ball arched across the corner of the box towards a loitering Scarinish attacker, Kieren rose to head it away – and succeeded only in directing it towards the top corner of the net.

It wasn't a goal only because Danny Loxham brought off one of his saves of the season. As the ball looped away from him Danny leapt frantically and with the tips of his fingers somehow managed to divert the ball over the bar even as he himself fell backwards into the net. By any standards, it was a breathtaking save and Kieren fell on the hero with undisguised relief. So, come to that, did most of the rest of the Kings present in the box. Sam just closed his eyes and made a mental note of action to be taken.

Happily for the Kings the corner came to

nothing and for a few moments the ball was removed from their penalty area.

Dominic Allenby would have preferred to run and run with it but his firm instructions from Sam were to 'stay in the back four, you're a defender now, not a midfielder.' So Dominic had to curb his attacking instincts and feed Foggy with a long and accurate pass. Foggy, too, remembered his orders to operate in midfield until told otherwise: so, with one touch he cleverly swept the ball on towards the pair up front.

Karl-Heinz was dreadfully unlucky. Anticipating the flight of the ball, he moved fast to trap it, turn and head for goal. But the ball bounced on a divot thrown up by a skid in a previous match and shot away at a sharp angle just as Karl-Heinz's foot was about to control it. So he was left stranded and looking, from the touchline, incompetent. Scarinish supporters weren't the only ones to jeer.

'Should have stayed in France, waste of time someone like him coming over here to play football,' remarked Melanie Todd's neighbour. 'Can't even *kick* the ball!'

Sam Saxton didn't say a word to anyone. Already he was wondering if he'd made the right decision to play the boy on the basis of the impressive work he'd done in one training session. Perhaps Karl was one of those who simply couldn't reproduce his practice game skills in the real thing: he couldn't cope with the pressure of real competition. There were plenty of youngsters like that and Sam had met his fair share of them in his career as a coach. This time, though, he had something to console him: if Karl-Heinz wasn't any good then at least he wouldn't be with the Kings for very long. The Kelly family said he'd be staying with them a maximum of three weeks.

Jakki wasn't prepared to write off her guest after one minor mistake. 'Come on, Karl, you can show 'em!' she called encouragingly. Kieren, who heard that, wished she'd show the same enthusiasm for *his* play. But then he had another thought: no, it was better if she kept quiet. Quite a few of his team-mates found it thoroughly irritating when parents were present and making a lot of noise. At the very least it was a distraction. It was bad enough having to try to impress the coach without being under the constant, critical scrutiny of their own family as well.

But Kieren couldn't dwell on that topic for Scarinish swarmed back into the Kings' box and once again Danny had to fling himself about like a sea-lion catching fish thrown by careless spectators. Joe Parbold and Dominic were the other rocks on which Scarinish attacks foundered whereas Kieren seemed unable to put a foot right. Inevitably, he made one mistake too many and when an attacker easily skipped over Kieren's hopeless tackle there was nothing this time that Danny could do to stop a shot fired in from point-blank range. So, within five minutes of the kick-off, the Goal Kings were one-down – and, what was more, looking distinctly jittery. As the boys in blue and black stripes celebrated with customary exuberance, Sam hurried along the touchline for a quick word. 'Just stay calm, Kieren. Don't worry and things'll come right. Just watch the ball. Never take your eyes off it.'

Kieren nodded that he'd heard and would do as he was told. Jakki, who'd also heard the advice, shot Sam a grateful glance. She'd watched enough coaches in action to know that another one might well have blasted Kieren into space for his mistakes in this game. She knew that Kieren would respond to the carrot, not the stick. It seemed Sam understood that, too.

Scarinish were naturally determined to double their lead as soon as possible. Having seen nothing of the Kings' attack to worry them, they believed the game would be theirs if they now threw more players forward to support their strikers. Accordingly, their defence was sharply reduced in numbers.

Next time Karl-Heinz got the ball, however, it hardly seemed to matter how many opponents were between him and the goalmouth. Pulling the ball down from a lobbed pass by Foggy, he rapidly switched it between his feet to bamboozle the first challenger and then picked up pace to swerve one way and dart the opposite way to fox the next adversary. Alex, who simply hadn't expected his co-striker to move so fast when he picked up the ball, had to sprint to be available for a pass. But the German had no intention of parting with the ball.

Now only one desperate defender stood between him and the goal-line. Karl-Heinz slowed up, pushed the ball just ahead of him as if tempting his opponent to come and take it, and the Scarinish boy couldn't resist the bait. The moment he committed himself, Karl-Heinz moved with the speed of a striking snake to flick the ball past him and into space. Just one obstacle remained between himself and the back of the net: a goalkeeper who didn't know whether to stay on his line or dash out to try to fling himself on to the ball. It didn't matter which he might have tried. For Karl-Heinz had picked his spot, the top right-hand corner of the net, and that's where he sent the ball. In spite of seeming to have no back-lift at all, he hit the ball with such power it went into the roof rigging with the force of a shell.

'Tremendous!'

'What a goal!'

'Unbelievable shot from that range!'

The praise rang round the ground from supporters and uncommitted spectators and even some Scarinish fans. Most, however, greeted the goal in stunned silence. For it was of a quality not many had witnessed at this level of competition.

Karl-Heinz himself treated the achievement in a fairly nonchalant manner, greeting the applause with a wave of the arm and then trying to fend off the mobbing by his teammates. Most of them recognized that it had done much more than just put them back in the game: it had shown that the skills they'd seen on the training pitch truly could be transplanted on to the real playing zone. Plainly his first attempted touch of the ball earlier was just a stroke of ill-luck. Karl-Heinz Bruggemann was the kind of instinctive goalscorer managers and coaches searched for all over the universe.

'How *did* you find him?' Sam Saxton enquired in awe-struck tones of Jakki Kelly who at that moment happened to be standing close by.

'Er, well, it's a long story,' she began cautiously. 'He can play, can't he?'

'Oh my goodness, I'll say so,' murmured Sam, still registering amazement. 'That certainly wasn't a fluke. Those skills are exceptional.'

Scarinish could hardly feel that it was a fluke, either, but nobody on their side seemed to suspect it might be repeated. So no immediate precautions were taken to close down Karl-Heinz so that he couldn't deal them another body blow. Only one of their recently moved midfielders dropped back a little as their coach urged his players to resume their all-out attack. He felt he had still seen nothing to convince him that Rodale Kings could win the points from this game. In particular, their defence appeared to be very ordinary with the thin, gangly full-back, Kieren, especially vulnerable under pressure.

But the next time Kieren was in action he pounced confidently on the ball to disarm a Scarinish attacker and neatly flick it sideways for Joe to complete the clearance. Sam's words of encouragement had been acted on at once and the coach nodded approvingly. Two minutes later he was applauding loudly along with practically every other Rodale supporter. For, after being 0–1 down, the Kings were 2–1 up.

This time it wasn't Karl-Heinz who put the ball in the net but it was he who set up the chance after taking a nicely judged pass from Lloyd Colmer on the right flank. Dragging the ball away from a sliding-in defender, Karl-Heinz then rounded another opponent with a sharply angled swerve before sending it with splendid precision for Alex to run on to and crash in a fierce shot. The goalkeeper got his hands to the ball but wasn't able to hold on to it. Alex, following up with his customary zeal in sight of goal, controlled the rebound and calmly steered the ball into the net. Alex's first reaction was to celebrate his triumph in front of the home supporters and then chase after Karl-Heinz to congratulate him. As appeared to be his style, the German player tried to shrug off the attentions of his team-mates as if to say that the goal really had nothing to do with him. Naturally, it had almost everything to do with him and the Rodale fans knew it.

So did the Scarinish coach. Belatedly, he set about reorganizing his defence to deal with the menace of the chubby, round-faced striker. He chose his toughest tackler to be his shadow throughout the rest of the game. It proved to be largely unnecessary for Karl-Heinz didn't get the ball once in the remainder of the first half, and in the second half he tended to lay the ball off the moment he received it and plainly began to fade from the action altogether as time ran out. During the interval Sam asked him how he was enjoying his first game in England and Karl-Heinz responded with one of his familiar hunching shrugs and said, 'OK, I suppose. We are winning, that is the important thing, ja?'

Nobody could argue with that but Sam was disappointed by the boy's seeming lack of effort in the second half, though once again he had a foot in the decisive third goal scored by Alex in a wild scramble after a corner kick. In fact, it was a back-heel from the German that allowed Alex to score with a tap-in. Sam thought of taking the boy off in the closing minutes with the Kings still leading 3–1 but he didn't want to disappoint him or the fans; and, of course, there was always a chance he might score another wonder goal.

'How're you feeling now, Karl-Heinz?'

Sam enquired anxiously after the final whistle for the boy looked drained.

'OK,' was the casual response. He wasn't going to admit that he felt almost exhausted but he did reveal: 'I may not be at my best. No game as long as this for almost a month. I may be out of practice. Is that how you say it?'

'I'm taking you off for a good meal, you must be starving,' said his hostess, Kieren's mum. 'It won't be just pancakes! You've got to have something more filling than that.'

Extra helpings at meal-times seemed to work the trick because in the next game, a Highlea Knock-out Cup-tie against Skeefling Swifts, Karl-Heinz appeared to possess much more energy. Possibly, too, he wanted to win another man-of-the-match award. Nobody could really deny that he deserved the first one, if only because of his 'wonder goal', as everyone now was describing it; yet Alex and his dad were still resentful that it hadn't gone to the player who'd now scored two goals in a match for the third time in succession and hadn't received a trophy for any of those feats. In Ricky Todd's mind, it suggested a conspiracy to deprive his son of his dues. If this were a professional game he'd be investigating the chances of getting a transfer to another club. Under the rules of the Highlea Sunday League, however, players weren't allowed to move from team to team during the season. They had to stick with the club that had signed them up even if they never got into the squad.

Skeefling had sailed through the previous round when they were up against a side that couldn't even raise eleven players for the game and so their supporters had high hopes for success again, especially as it was known that Rodale Kings had only crept past Clocklane in a penalty shoot-out. They hadn't heard about Karl-Heinz and so had no idea what he was capable of anywhere near the penalty area. They soon found out. In only the third minute of the game the stocky striker intercepted a pass intended for someone else by taking the ball on his instep; from there he flicked it up on to his knee for a single bounce and then, swivelling with surprising speed, hit a left-foot shot that simply screamed into the top corner of the net with the entire

Skeefling defence practically transfixed.

Even the referee couldn't resist applauding a demonstration of skill that he'd never seen before at this level of play. The Rodale fans were excited enough to invade the pitch – well just trespass over the touchline – until officials shooed them back with dire warnings. Sam Saxton simply couldn't stop smiling. During the training session earlier that week Karl-Heinz had looked neither slimmer nor particularly interested in what was being attempted, which was in stark contrast to the display of his skills he'd put on the first time he'd turned up. Could it be that he was just *bored* by what they'd been practising? Well, Sam conceded, that was possible. After all, no one else in the squad could do the tricks Karl-Heinz performed so fluently.

It took the gold-shirted Swifts several minutes to recover from the shock of that goal; and by then they were two-down. Foggy Thrale was the scorer this time, hooking in a low-level cross from Alex that Karl-Heinz deliberately missed. His dummy completely flummoxed the defence and so Foggy had a very clear sight of the target.

Because he had been building up to a moment like this in his private training he was confident he'd score. He did. Then, only ten minutes later, the still-shaken defence reacted quite pathetically to another full-scale Rodale attack when a full-back feebly headed the ball right into the path of Lloyd who might have found it easier to fly a plane than miss this opening. He didn't. Skeefling Swifts 0, Rodale Goal Kings 3 was the half-time score.

In the second half Skeefling produced some stern defending and occasional good moves in midfield but couldn't prevent Rodale scoring two more, the first a close-range header from Karl-Heinz, the second a well-placed drive past an out-of-position keeper by Alex, who shortly afterwards had to go off with an ankle injury. In spite of his second goal Karl-Heinz didn't shine after the interval and once again Sam was left to wonder whether the German boy could really last out a full game. Still, there wouldn't be much point in finding the answer to that riddle because Karl-Heinz would be returning home after the next League match. Meanwhile, the really important point was that the Kings were in the next round of the Cup. So Sam was still beaming as the final whistle sounded on a 5–0 triumph. Today, the Goal Kings had lived up their name.

Ricky Todd was experiencing mixed emotions. His pleasure in the victory was tempered by his concern at Alex's latest injury. His son certainly got more than his fair share of knocks, doubtless, Ricky felt, because of his speed on the ball and his pace generally. It was ironic that Karl-Heinz, who was nowhere near as fast as Alex, didn't appear to get kicked or suffer any strains in spite of being closely marked. Moreover, he had no doubt at all that Karl-Heinz would again collect the man-of-the-match award for *his* two goals. So Alex was unlucky yet again.

As the players disappeared into the changing-rooms for hot showers before setting off in the minibus back to Rodale Kings, Ricky also pondered the problem of what to do now about his plans to take over as coach. After this run of success Sam was in a stronger position than ever. Perhaps only a few of the parents Ricky had talked to so earnestly about the future would be willing to agree to a change. Yet weaknesses in the team were still obvious and Sam was as obsessed by defending in depth rather than attacking with flair. If Karl-Heinz wasn't there who in the present squad was good enough to support Alex up front? There was only one answer: no one.

And, very soon, Karl-Heinz *wouldn't* be there any more. That would be the real testing time for the present squad.

Ricky, too, now managed a smile. Perhaps he wouldn't have to wait so long, after all.

Foggy Thrale leapt high, waited for the perfect moment and smashed the shuttlecock beyond Danny Loxham's reach. Or, at least, he thought he had. But Danny, ever the amazing athlete, somehow got across the court and, with his racket at full stretch, managed to flick it back over the net.

It was all to no avail. Anticipating the direction of any possible return, Foggy was at the net to thwack the shuttle downwards for a killing point even as Danny was still scrambling to his feet. 'Yes!' Foggy congratulated himself with an air-punching gesture. 'Six-nil now, Dan. You ought to surrender. You'll never get back into the game against me.'

'Pity he doesn't hit so many winners on the footie pitch,' observed Alex Todd drily as he sipped a drink at the table he was sharing with some of his team-mates in the carpeted viewing area behind a badminton court at Rodale leisure centre.

'Yeah, but to be fair, he is getting better,' said Joe Parbold. 'Must be our most improved player this season, along with Dominic.'

'Must be the only ones then, considering the way we've been playing recently,' Josh Rowley commented cynically. As he wasn't in the team very often he felt he could risk that kind of remark because no one could honestly assess his form. They didn't know about his private relentless training sessions.

It wasn't disputed. It was in the minds of all of them that the Kings were having the worst run of results any of them had ever experienced in the League. Since Karl-Heinz's departure, when he signed off with another spectacular goal, an overhead scissors kick, they hadn't won a single game, although two matches had been lost by the narrowest margin. What everyone supporting one side or the other regarded as 'The Grudge Match', the game against Clocklane Strikers, their first Cup victims, had proved to be a disaster.

Marcus, the Strikers' bustling hero, had notched a hat-trick, although one of the goals he claimed had been put into his own net by Joe, always called 'The Rock' by Sam. On this occasion a bit of him had crumbled away when he diverted a fierce free kick out of Danny's reach.

Sam kept making changes to deal with what he and several parents admitted was a crisis. Yet again, though, it was the defence that concerned him most and so he kept tinkering with it, drafting in, and out again, players like Josh and Frazer McKinnon, a Scot whose family had only recently arrived in the village. Frazer was in the Joe Parbold mould but at present he lacked Joe's positional sense and strength; even when he was in the right place he was forced off the ball too easily by determined attackers. Dominic Allenby had slotted in alongside Joe and that was the most permanent arrangement in the team. With the exception, of course, of Danny in goal. But he wasn't there just because of Sam's favouritism: Danny scarcely ever made a blunder and his saves sometimes bordered on the miraculous. On the other hand, when those in front of Danny made horrendous errors, as happened all too frequently in a couple of games, even his abilities weren't enough to prevent goals being scored. The attack wasn't performing brilliantly, either. When things went wrong everyone remembered Karl-Heinz and pointed out that he was irreplaceable. And on that sad note the comments usually ended.

'I can't be expected to do *everything* on my own,' Alex would protest, forgetting that before Karl-Heinz's arrival he had claimed he could. His ankle injury was still bothering him and he'd missed three League matches. So, of course, he wasn't at all surprised that the Kings hadn't been able to win in his absence. Ricky took the same view.

'You've got to find another striker, Sam, got to,' he told the coach. Sam, nodding, said he was always on the look-out for new talent and for a couple of matches brought in Davey Stroud who hadn't been picked up by any other Sunday League team although he'd scored a hatful of goals in school matches. But Davey, not very tall though with a rare ability to reach high crosses, didn't find the net on behalf of the Kings.

Happily, the team kept winning in the Knock-out Cup and luck really seemed to be on their side. Their goals came from a variety of sources with no fewer than four being scored by generous opponents. In Alex's absence, Joe converted all three penalties the Kings were awarded, two of them being distinctly dubious refereeing decisions, and Lloyd Colmer proved to be a successful replacement for Alex. In the quarter-final they'd been drawn at home to a team they'd already beaten easily in the League. This time it was a scrappy match but the Kings scraped through 2–1 with the winning goal being struck from the penalty spot by Joe with only two minutes of normal time remaining.

Alex was back for the semi-final – another home tie – against Bankhouse Invaders, a team little was known about as they were newcomers to the Highlea League and played in a different division. The Invaders lived up to their name by attacking zestfully in the early stages of the match, a ploy that Rodale were by now very familiar with and one which Sam was sure they could handle.

Rumours began to spread around the ground that Bankhouse had three of their best players missing because of a vicious flu virus that was circulating; and eventually it became obvious that the entire team was running out of energy. When two players had to be taken off because they were feeling unwell only one substitute was fit enough to take their places. So, without having to work very hard, the Kings comfortably won 3–0 against a tired team that finished with only ten players.

'Our name must be on the Cup!' Danny gloated as they left the pitch. 'We're in unstoppable form.'

Not many believed that; and, when the Kings' form dipped again in the League, the dark mutterings among parents turned to calls for changes. Ricky found it very difficult not to reply 'I told you so' when people said to him that something had to be done to improve the attack, to provide Alex with the support he deserved. The boys themselves, or several of them, at least, were starting to worry about what might happen if their luck ran out when the Cup Final was played early in the New Year. Whenever they gathered together, as some of them were doing now for some friendly badminton just as the Christmas holidays were beginning, the talk soon drifted to football.

'Hey, Alex, is it true that your dad is trying to take over the team?' asked Josh without any warning. 'If he does, well, he'll want to make changes, won't he?'

Before Alex could decide how to answer that, Joe, frowning, said, 'I haven't heard about that. Where'd you hear that, Josher? And what's wrong with Sam as the Boss? He *is* the Boss, the best I've ever seen.'

At that moment Foggy executed a kind of war dance to celebrate his victory over Danny and then dashed across the court to join the other boys. It was impossible for him to miss the worried expressions on several faces. 'Hey, fellas, what's up? I mean, what am I missing?'

'Alex is just going to tell us if it's true that his dad is going to be the Kings' new coach,' Joe kindly explained.

'What!' exclaimed Foggy and Danny simultaneously. Their minds immediately fast-forwarded to what such a change might mean for them personally. Danny, knowing how much the coach favoured him, was the first to a question. 'Has Sam packed up? Or is he going to another team?'

Alex shook his head irritably and brushed his eyebrows fiercely. 'No, no, nothing's fixed. It's only a rumour – I think. I know Dad would like to be the coach but nothing's been done about it so far as I know.'

'But he'd make changes, wouldn't he?' Foggy said eagerly. '*All* new coaches do their own thing, look at teams in a different way from the guy who was there before them. So Mr Todd would do the same!'

'I suppose so,' Alex admitted. 'But, honestly, guys, nothing's going on at present, I'm sure. Anyway, it wouldn't happen before Christmas because that's too close. Dad's got other things on his mind.' He paused and then a joke occurred to him. 'Like Christmas presents! Hope he's getting something good for me.'

'But he won't need a new goalkeeper,' Danny declared with his usual confidence. 'I mean, I *am* the best, you know that. I instil confidence in the entire defence, that's what Sam says.'

'Yeah, but if Sam's not there to say it, if he's gone, well, maybe another coach won't think you're so brilliant,' said Foggy, always envious of Danny's position as Sam the Slammer's favourite player.

'Listen, Alex, you know your dad talks a lot to my mum, don't you?' Josh suddenly asked without realizing the effect his words could have on the rest of the boys.

'Oh yeah? Oh, tell us more. What's that supposed to mean, Josh, that Mr Todd fancies Mrs Rowley?' they broke in with varying degrees of amusement and romantic interest.

'No, no, nothing like that. Honestly, you've got one-track minds, you guys. No, what I mean is, Mr Todd *knows* I don't get a fair deal from Sam. My mum thinks that and, well, Mr Todd thinks the same. So if he becomes the coach he'll want me in the team, won't he? So, Alex, make sure he knows I'm, er, *available*.'

Joe hadn't said anything for a little while because something mentioned earlier was still preying on his mind. Now he voiced it. 'Rich men like to give themselves presents, don't they? Especially for Christmas. So is this what your dad's doing, Alex, buying himself a football team so that he can play with it like, well, like a new toy?'

Alex was flabbergasted by that suggestion. 'Rich! We're not rich. OK, Dad owns a furniture factory but that's all. That doesn't make you rich. Only means he has to work hard to look after the jobs of his workers. Anyway, who said anything about *buying* a team? There'd be no money involved. Sam doesn't own the Kings so money wouldn't be changing hands, would it? Oh, and Dad doesn't have to give himself a present. Mum and I give him presents.'

Kieren Kelly hadn't said a word as the rest of the players had their discussion. He'd simply sipped his drink and chewed on a gooey chocolate bar. Now he spoke. 'D'you know what I'd like for Christmas?' he enquired, though without waiting for a reply. 'I'd like Karl-Heinz to come back and play for us again. Then I'd get into the team regularly and I'd also get as many of his pancakes as I could eat. They're out of this world, like his football.'

For some moments no one made any

response at all as they thought about the implications of that idea. Then Joe, his eyes lighting up with rare excitement, exclaimed, 'Great idea, that, Kieren. Because then Karl-Heinz could make sure we win the Knockout Cup next month!'

8 Party Time

'Well, this is all very pleasant, I must say,' remarked Jane Allenby to Jakki Kelly as she sipped a glass of white wine and looked round the crowded sitting-room at the home of Melanie and Ricky Todd. 'Nice way to welcome in the New Year even if it is a few hours away yet.'

Jakki nodded. 'The invitation was a surprise, I've got to admit. Haven't been here before. But there must be another reason for this little gathering – well, not so little really. Ricky only does things for a purpose, I'm told, so I wonder what's in his cunning mind.'

That purpose became crystal clear later in the evening when he asked the Kings' parents and closest supporters to join him for 'just a few minutes to talk about something important. No one will interrupt us in the TV room on the other side of the dining-room,' said their host. No one remarked on the absence of Sam Saxton but after hearing Ricky's opening words everyone knew precisely why the coach hadn't been invited.

'Look, I don't want to make a meal out of this so I'll be very brief. Don't want to spoil any New Year parties you may be going on to later,' he added with a rather nervous smile. 'The point is, as you all know the Kings have been having a bad time, hardly winning a game except in the Cup. Well, if we don't take action now we could be relegated come April. We can't have that. End of all our dreams that would be. So I'm proposing we take a decisive step tonight: ask Sam Saxton to stand down as coach. Replace him before the next match. I've talked to a few of you about this already so now I need to know: does anybody disagree? Anybody think this is a wrong move for the team, *our* team?'

For several moments there was complete silence as various people either exchanged quick glances with one another or stared rather woodenly at paintings on the wall or even at the blank face of the huge TV set. Jakki wished that someone would speak up first, someone bigger and more forceful than herself, but when no one did she knew her allies were relying on her.

'Who would take his place, Ricky?' she asked in as neutral a voice as possible. 'Have you got anyone in mind apart from yourself?'

Clearly Ricky hadn't expected such a direct challenge from someone he'd thought of as one of his likely supporters. 'Well, I'd be willing to do the job, of course. I feel I am qualified and I've helped out quite a bit at training sessions. Also, we don't want to bring in a complete stranger at this stage of the season, do we? That would hardly be fair on the boys.'

'Is it the boys you're thinking about most, or your own position?' Jakki pressed on relentlessly.

'Oh, come on, Jakki, this isn't just about personalities, this is about the team, *our* team, as I said,' Ricky replied, sounding exasperated or annoyed or probably both.

'That's right, but it's the boys themselves we've got to think of first, think of what's right for them, what's *best* for them,' declared Joe's mum, Tracie Parbold. Her husband,

Steve, standing beside her, nodded briskly. 'You see, Ricky, we've been talking about this, too. They've heard all sorts of whispers and a lot of them are worried, worried about what might happen if you replaced Sam. They fear Alex may be made captain and that there'd be other changes. No – no – please let me finish, Ricky. You see, boys of their age don't really like change. They like to stick to what they know. They may not all like Sam but they trust him, they know he's always doing his best for the *entire* team.'

'Hear, hear,' one or two people murmured audibly.

'He's also very thoughtful, is Sam,' Jakki resumed. 'When Kieren didn't play well against Scarinish, Sam took the trouble to talk him through the problem and then give him another chance. So Kieren feels he's learning, even if he isn't always in the team. Oh yes, and of course Sam took a chance with Karl-Heinz. Let's face it, he didn't know that Karl-Heinz could play as he did against Scarinish and then Skeefling. None of us did.'

'But that's just one example,' Ricky tried to retaliate. 'Over-all, he just thinks defensively, doesn't bother much about the forwards. We've got to have more striking power. We've got to score *goals*, live up to our name. Surely we can all see that?'

'Yes, we do know that,' said Serena Colmer. 'Ricky, I want to ask you something. Do you know what the players have been up to since, well, before Christmas? Has your Alex told you what they're trying to do?'

'Er, I'm not sure,' Ricky conceded, looking genuinely puzzled. 'I don't think that Alex has many, er, secrets from me where the team is concerned.'

'Well, they've been raising every penny they can to try and pay for Karl-Heinz to come over to play for us in the Cup Final, that's what they've been up to,' Serena revealed with a broad smile. 'They've been cleaning cars, shopping for neighbours, tidying gardens, you name it, they've done it if there's a penny to be made. I'm just surprised Alex hasn't told you, Ricky.'

'I have been very busy lately with my work,' Ricky said weakly. 'Maybe I just didn't listen to him when I should've done. But that's not on, is it, bringing him from

Bordeaux just for one match? Even if he were free, even if his family would allow it. So –'

'Oh, Karl-Heinz's dad doesn't mind at all,' Jakki announced. 'I know, I've talked to him on the phone. But he's ploughed all his money into his new restaurant so he can't afford to fund his son's trip. Karl-Heinz himself would *love* to return for the weekend. Just like every other player, he'd love to win a medal in a Cup Final. A *winner's* medal, naturally.'

'Well, I see that,' said Ricky, plainly taken aback by the news of what had been going on and by the attitude of the people who were speaking against his idea of a takeover. 'So how is the, er, fund-raising going? Have you got as much as you need?'

'Well, I think we're getting there,' Steve Parbold said. 'But air fares are expensive if you aren't flying on a package deal. That's the big item because Clark and Jakki are kindly putting Karl-Heinz up at their place again.'

'Oh, count me in, please,' Ricky offered quickly, seeing a chance to gain some much-needed support. 'I'd be delighted to chip in, make up any shortfall. I'd certainly do that. After all, he and Alex formed a really good partnership up-front, didn't they? So it'd be great to think they could team up again for the Final.'

'Ricky, he'd be good for the *whole* team,' Tracie pointed out. 'And, you know, that's the way Sam thinks. He's concerned about everyone. That's –'

'Oh, but so does Ricky, he wants all the Kings' boys to do well,' Melanie cut in, thinking it was time she displayed some support for her husband. 'Tracie, I know how Ricky thinks and I know he deeply, genuinely wants only the best for the team, not just Alex.'

Ricky wished she hadn't added those last three words because they served to remind everyone that he was bound to have mixed emotions if things were going badly for Alex in any particular game and he himself were the coach.

'I'm sure he does,' said Jakki. She recognized that the discussion, if it could be called that, was generally in favour of her point of view. She could afford to be magnanimous and so she flashed a quick smile at the Todds.

'But most of us think – well, I'm sure it's most of us – Sam has done pretty well for the team. On the eve of a Cup Final I don't think we can possibly consider replacing the man who has got the team there.'

Once again several listeners voiced their support with 'Hear, hear.'

Ricky realized it would be foolish to take a vote, which was what he'd had in mind. His defeat would be inevitable. People would remember it and therefore he might never have another chance of getting what he wanted so much.

'Well, if that's how most people feel, fine, let's accept that point of view,' Ricky said as graciously as possible. 'As we're *all* agreed, the success of the team must come first. We've all got to work for that together. After all, we do want that Cup, don't we?'

'Definitely!' Clark Kelly declared. 'And with that brilliant German boy in our side I'm positive we're going to win it.'

That was quite clearly the note on which to finish the informal meeting in the Todds' TV room and quite soon afterwards all the guests had departed for their own homes or

New Year's Eve parties elsewhere. All were in a cheerful mood.

'Well, I have to confess I've lost a battle,' Ricky Todd said to Melanie when they were alone again. Then the sad note in his voice changed to one of optimism. 'But I haven't lost the war. Next time I'll be better prepared. And *I'll* win.'

9 The Final Touch

'I feel like a big star!' Karl-Heinz exclaimed, wide-eyed, as he looked around him at the airport. Flashes were exploding on cameras pointed at him and everyone who wasn't carrying a camera was waving and crying, 'Welcome back, welcome back!'

'Well, you are a star, in our eyes,' smiled Jakki Kelly as she gave him a hug. She wanted to kiss him but feared that would embarrass him in front of some of his teammates. 'I expect the local paper will be at the match, so you'll get some more of the star treatment from them. They're very impressed that you're flying in from France just for one game. They've already given us some publicity because we all raised money for your air fare and so on. In fact, the whole village now seems to be supporting the Kings. But you are going to be the centre of attention.

Everybody'll want to see you in action.'

'Then I must not let you down,' he replied with a half-smile and a lift of his eyebrows.

'You won't do that, Karl-Heinz, you'll win the match for us, no doubt about that,' Kieren told him as they climbed into the minibus for the journey to the town ground where the Highlea Sunday League Knock-Out Cup Final was being staged. 'Then we'll go home and you can make us your famous pancakes to celebrate! Can't wait to taste them again.'

'Hey, make some for us, too, Karl-Heinz,' Danny Loxham requested eagerly. '*Please*. Be great if the whole team could be there. Would that be all right, Mrs Kelly?'

'I should think so,' she replied, though not sounding entirely convincing. 'Be a perfect way to celebrate a very special day, I agree.'

'Just as long as we do win,' added Clark Kelly cautiously from the driver's seat. 'D'you know what my worry was today? That the air traffic controllers would be on strike again and so Karl-Heinz's plane wouldn't get here on time, or wouldn't get here at all. That would have ruined the Final for us, wouldn't it?'

165

Originally it had been arranged that Karl-Heinz's visit to play in the Cup Final should begin on the evening before the match; but then an industrial dispute involving air traffic staff had meant the cancellation of most flights that day. Everyone connected with the Goal Kings was horrified. After all the time and effort and generosity that had gone into setting up the trip it appeared that their hoped-for hero would be stranded at home! Then, at the eleventh hour, an agreement had been reached and normal flights were resumed. Nonetheless, it meant that Karl-Heinz couldn't possibly land in England much more than an hour before the Final was due to kick-off. Hence the relief at the local airport when his plane touched down and Karl-Heinz emerged with the rest of the passengers.

'Have you been playing a lot in France, Karl-Heinz?' Danny enquired as Mr Kelly negotiated an awkward roundabout close to the town ground. 'I mean, are you in top form, *goal-scoring* form? This lot we're playing in the Final are supposed to have a terrific defence. So Sam says we need somebody special to unlock it!'

The German boy shook his head. 'Very little, I must tell you. At Christmas and New Year the players seem to have a holiday, too. But I have been training on my own. I feel fine.'

'Good!' Kieren and Danny exclaimed simultaneously in relief.

'Who is this team we play?' Karl-Heinz wanted to know as everyone began to clamber out of the minibus which had parked on the wide forecourt in front of the town ground, by far the biggest stadium in the region. None of the Kings had ever played there before on any occasion and part of the excitement of reaching the Knock-out Cup Final was the chance to play on a famous pitch.

'Friday Bridge, they're called,' Danny replied. 'Not United or Strikers or Colts or anything like that. Their fans just call 'em The Bridge.'

'Strange name, ja?'

'Suppose so, when you think about it. A mate of mine who used to play for them says they got the name because when the village was being built they needed a bridge across the river. This was, oh, centuries ago and everyone was so busy putting up the houses and stuff they hadn't time to make a bridge as well. Then it was decided everybody who could help build it should put every Friday aside just for that job. So that's why it got its name. It's only a footbridge and it's still a pretty small village. Some of the team come from other places near by. It's got a really good record, you see.'

'Sounds like you ought to be their publicity officer, Danny!' remarked Sam Saxton, who'd overheard some of the story. 'But don't you be giving them any goals as well as that free publicity. Remember you're in goal to win the game for us.'

He turned to Karl-Heinz and held out his hand. 'Good to have you back with us, Karl-Heinz. Thanks for coming all this way just for one match. The Kings really appreciate it, I can tell you.'

Karl-Heinz nodded. 'I also like to see my friends. Kieren is my friend.'

Kieren glowed. Although he knew his play was improving he was by no means sure of his place in the side on a regular basis so it helped enormously that Karl-Heinz declared such support for him. For there wasn't any doubt that Sam and the Kings needed the German boy to be in the best of moods and win the game for them. In recent matches it had been evident that the Kings weren't functioning well, especially in attack.

'You'll be able to resume your old partnership with Alex,' Sam was continuing. 'We've got another pretty useful striker since you were with us, a boy called Davey Stroud. But Davey's not developed your skills on the ball yet, so he'll be one of the subs today.'

Alex, who'd come across to join in the welcome to Karl-Heinz but wasn't going to interrupt Sam's comments, guessed that the reference to Davey was mainly intended for his ears. Alex knew he himself was on trial at present, mostly because of his failure to score in recent matches. For some inexplicable reason his early season form had deserted him. So he, too, needed to be touched by Karl-Heinz's magic. But if things didn't go his way then he had no doubt Sam the Slammer would close the door on him by replacing him with the crop-haired, bouncy and ever-alert Davey Stroud.

'How's the ankle, Alex?' Sam enquired as the players assembled in the changing-room which was at least twice as large as any they'd used previously. 'No reaction from this week's training stint?'

'No, it's fine, Boss. Can't feel a thing,' Alex quickly assured him. Lately he'd adopted Joe's form of address to the coach, partly because he believed it might help him to remain in favour. Since his dad's failure to take over Sam's role Alex had worried about his own place in the team.

'Sam's bound to know all about the meeting we had at our place because you can't keep secrets in a village like this,' Ricky had warned him. 'But Sam won, if you want to call it that, so he won't have any reason to treat you differently in future.'

Alex wasn't sure about any of that because he knew that some people didn't reveal their secrets and it seemed to him that Sam never praised him for anything he did on or off the pitch. He sensed that the coach would simply drop him from the squad altogether if only he could unearth another quality striker. Meanwhile, his questions about Alex's niggling knocks and injuries served only to undermine Alex's confidence in his ability to last out a game. But if he could put on a brilliant performance in the Cup Final, rounding it off maybe with the winning goal, then his future in the team ought to be guaranteed, especially as Karl-Heinz would be returning home the next day, probably never to return to Rodale.

'So, come on, Alex, come *on*!' he muttered to himself under his breath as he pulled up his white shorts and tucked in the Kings' distinctive purple shirt with white trim. 'This is the biggest match of your life, so shine, shine. Be the biggest star!'

'You OK, Alex?' inquired Dominic who was sitting alongside him and was always slower to get changed. He still hadn't put his socks on because he was rubbing some liniment into his shins.

'Yeah, I'm fine. Why're you asking?'

'Oh, well, I thought you looked a bit worked-up, that's all,' Dominic replied mildly.

'I expect everybody is,' Alex continued

aggressively. 'This is the Cup Final, you know. You're wound up as well, I'll bet.'

'Suppose so,' Dominic agreed. 'But I have an easier job because *their* defence is the strong part of the team, not the attack. So *our* attack has to work harder. Good job we've got Karl-Heinz to –'

'Listen, what about me?' Alex burst out. 'I've scored most goals for the Kings this season, not Karl-Heinz. He hasn't been here most of the time. Even if he had been, I'd still have been the leading scorer. So –'

'OK, OK, sorry I said the wrong thing,' Dominic offered placatingly. He put the liniment away and started to draw on his hooped socks. 'Alex, I hope you score loads of goals today so that we win the Cup. That's the only thing that matters.'

Alex looked round to see if anyone had been listening to their exchanges. He realized he could easily have upset Karl-Heinz or, worse still, Sam. However, both of them were involved in other conversations.

'What is that stuff? It's got a real pong,' he said to Dominic in a friendly tone. He didn't want to fall out, either, with the Kings' most improved player of the season, one who, like Danny, seemed always to be in favour with the coach.

'Some liniment my mum swears by. Says it's perfect for relaxing your muscles and making them supple. You know, she's really got quite keen on football and she's coming to watch us today. If she gets close enough to me she'll be able to smell I've got it on. Want to try some, Alex?'

'Er, no thanks,' replied the team's top striker. 'My muscles are all in pretty good shape.'

As if to prove the point he jumped to his feet and went into a routine of rhythmical bouncing, jumping and body-swinging exercises. This had become a habit before the start of every game even though he worried sometimes he might overdo it when he had to nurse a recent knock or sprain. The important thing was to convince Sam that his fitness was beyond question.

Then, when he trotted out with the rest of the team, his father, standing on the touch-line, enquired anxiously, 'How're you feeling now?'

Alex groaned inwardly and through clenched teeth muttered, 'Fine, just fine!' He glanced round to see whether Sam was within earshot but the coach was deep in conversation with his opposite number. To no one's surprise, Ricky Todd was on his own – even Melanie hadn't turned up yet. Although Ricky had kept his promise to pay a sizeable sum for the remainder of Karl-Heinz's travel costs the other Kings' parents and devoted supporters seemed wary of socializing with him now. It was as if he'd been branded a traitor because he'd attempted to take Sam's job from him.

Yet Ricky didn't really mind; it was much as he'd expected. In his view he'd made out a good case for the removal of Sam and people would remember that if the Kings failed to win the Cup. After all, they'd continued to perform poorly in the League and so their whole season really rested on victory today. Sam, therefore, was on trial. Within the next couple of hours the verdict would be known.

'Hey, that's a dazzy sort of outfit,' Foggy exclaimed as the Friday Bridge team appeared in their red and yellow shirts designed, harlequin-style, in lots of little squares and matching red shorts.

'We *always* beat teams in bright colours,' Danny pointed out. 'Remember Clocklane Strikers in their orange outfits? Well, we outshone them all right!'

'But only in a penalty shoot-out,' said Joe Parbold, still haunted by his own miss from the spot in that game. 'Hope we don't have to go through all that again.'

'Doesn't worry me,' said Alex, quickly regaining his usual confidence. 'I'll still be on the pitch this time to bang in the first penalty; none of that lot over there are going to get me sent off in this game. This is my day to grab some goals. And Karl-Heinz is going to hit a few, too. Right, Karl-Heinz?'

The German just shrugged because he hadn't really been listening; his attention was focused on the baize-covered table between the dug-outs where a large silver trophy and rows of glittering medals were on view. Sam spotted his interest and, summoning the rest of the players towards him, pointed at the prizes. 'They're what you're playing for, boys. So go on and win 'em for my sake. For the team's sake. For the Kings!'

They grinned and raised thumbs and fists in anticipation of their triumph. Alex, who'd earlier in the season concluded that Rodale wouldn't win anything, had begun to change his mind, not least because of the return of Karl-Heinz. Even without him, however, the Kings had managed to win through previous rounds of the Cup to reach the Final. So with the German playing today as his co-striker their chances of success had risen sharply. The hardness of the pitch after recent severe frosts wouldn't help his ankle but he wasn't going to give in to any discomfort. Like all his team-mates, he wanted to be a winner.

Friday Bridge kicked off and soon whipped the ball back to their vaunted defence to pass around among themselves as if to test its qualities and perhaps their own footwear on what would be a difficult surface. Alex and Karl-Heinz were under orders to exert pressure on opponents from the outset and so they dived in to try to gain possession. These opponents, however, were well used to dealing with unscientific challenges and so managed to steer the ball away to safety. Alex took a vicious jab in the ribs from one crafty bit of elbowing but somehow managed to restrain himself from retaliating. Karl-Heinz wasn't so lucky. A kick on the thigh when he stumbled after an attempt at a ball-winning tackle left him in pain and angry. Fortunately, he missed the target completely when he swung his arm at the perpetrator. The ref, well up with play, saw the incident and whistled instantly.

'Try that again, son, and you'll be off this pitch immediately,' he told the German. 'I know your blow didn't land but the intention was crystal clear. Violent conduct of that kind isn't allowed in *my* matches.'

Karl-Heinz, still rubbing his thigh vigorously to ease the pain, didn't argue. His control of his temper was the equal of his control of the ball. All the same, he made a mental note of the identity of his abusive opponent and would get his own back when the opportunity to do so unseen occurred.

'Come on, you Kings, you're getting no-where!' yelled Jakki Kelly, echoing the sense

177

of frustration of many of their supporters. 'Get at 'em!'

Her criticism was aimed at the forwards because the defence, where Kieren was in the back four, simply hadn't been tested yet, Friday Bridge being content to take command of the middle of the pitch. But that rallying cry seemed to act as a stimulus to the opposition and suddenly attackers in red and yellow shirts swarmed forward with the left-winger then sending over a teasing cross that Joe managed to clear only at the expense of giving away a corner kick.

'You should have come out for that,' he told Danny and the goalkeeper didn't deny it. He'd thought the ball was further from him than it was.

Fortunately, the corner kick came to nothing because Danny was able to punch the ball away and Kieren completed the clearance. The Kings' attack, however, failed to function effectively when they did manage to set up an attack. For once, Karl-Heinz under-hit his pass to Alex, principally because he was still suffering from his thigh strain. Alex had to stretch to have any hope of getting the ball and that was when an opponent clattered into him. Pain flared in the ankle again when he got to his feet and it was just as well the Bridge player had moved out of reach. Worse, he had the ball and was setting up another attack.

'Sorry!' Karl-Heinz signalled. Alex gritted his teeth against the quality of the pass as well as the pain and then began to wonder if he'd be able to continue if the twinges didn't go away. The very last thing he wanted was to be substituted; if Davey came on and scored then Alex might never get back into the team. It was vital that he himself scored at least once and made a major contribution to the Kings' victory. His luck, though, seemed to be right out these days.

Moments later several players and fans alike felt the team's luck was right out, too. For when Friday Bridge's speedy left-winger floated in another clever cross there was a sickening clash of heads between Joe and Kieren when they both went for the ball; and both collapsed motionless in the penalty area. Luckily, Danny was there to scoop up the loose ball before any attacker could get to it and then, when he saw that his team-mates plainly needed attention, he booted it over the touchline.

The referee stopped the game at once and one or two spectators followed Sam on to the pitch to see what needed to be done. Alex was quite grateful for the interlude which he could spend massaging his foot in the hope of making it better. Jane Allenby, who was on the touchline close by, watched him for a moment before calling to him.

'Alex, come over here and let me see if I can help. I might have something for you.'

Without hesitation he left the pitch and went to sit on the grass facing her while she slipped off her shoulder bag and then unzipped it. He knew, of course, that Dominic's mum was a nurse and so he patiently awaited her exploration of his ankle after she'd rolled down his sock. Her touch was gentle but he still bit his lip when she found the trouble-some area.

'Hang on, Alex,' she said. 'Think I've got the right thing to put on this ankle.'

'It's not that awful-smelling ointment, is it?' he asked, alarmed.

She laughed. 'No, it's a support bandage. It'll help ease some of the pressure on your foot. I always carry some medical aids for emergencies when I'm out. And I think your condition during a Cup Final can be classified as an emergency, don't you?'

As soon as he got to his feet he could tell that the comforting bandage had improved matters. He could move more easily. 'Thanks, Mrs Allenby,' he said. 'Feels great.'

Things were better in the penalty area, too, where Kieren and Joe were also on their feet, although Joe still looked a little dazed. Although the subs had been warming up, Sam said they weren't needed for the present.

'But I'll be watching out for our wounded to see whether there are any lasting effects,' he told the Parbold and Kelly families. 'They say they're all right but then nobody wants to come off in a Cup Final.'

Within two minutes, however, Joe made a thoroughly uncharacteristic error of judgement when tackling an opponent just inside the box. He would complain afterwards that he was simply going for the ball but the challenge was clumsy enough to send the

Bridge attacker tumbling. When he rolled to his knees his first words were, 'Penalty! Must be!'

The ref agreed with him.

'Oh no!' Joe moaned, sinking his bruised head into his hands. It didn't occur to him that probably he was still suffering from that collision with Kieren but that was the view of practically every Rodale supporter present.

Moments later the Friday Bridge supporters in the large crowd were ecstatic. Fittingly it was the left-winger who took the kick and drove the ball out of Danny's reach into the roof of the net. Joe appeared inconsolable as his team-mates tried to assure him he wasn't to blame for the goal; it was a display of unity that heartened Sam as he clapped his hands to urge his players: 'Just get on with the game. It's only a hiccup.'

Even if it was only a hiccup it occurred at a bad time, a minute before half-time, and thus there was no realistic opportunity for the Kings to snatch the equalizer. Sam repeated his confident words during the interval, stressing his view that Bridge had really offered no threat until they'd luckily gained the penalty. Now they'd probably just try to sit on their lead and that would provide the Kings' attack with ample chances to get forward and lay siege to their goalmouth. It did cross his mind, though he wasn't going to mention it, that Bridge just might try to double their lead immediately the game restarted in the hope that two goals would be enough to win the game.

In fact, they fell back into their well-marshalled defensive formation and so Alex and Karl-Heinz, backed up by Foggy and Lloyd, were able to run at them almost at will. But nothing they tried quite worked. Karl-Heinz's timing seemed to be awry at crucial moments and his shooting was simply woeful on both occasions he had a clear sight of the goal. That couldn't be put down to his thigh strain, he knew; for some reason, he just wasn't on his usual form. Alex, too, had nothing to complain about physically because the support bandage was doing its job and he experienced no real discomfort from his ankle.

'Alex, go *wider*. Their central defenders won't move out, so you'll have more space on the wings,' Ricky advised his son during a momentary stoppage while a Bridge player was receiving treatment after a fall on a patch as firm as a rock.

That plot almost worked immediately. After picking up a loose ball from a midfield mêlée Alex darted off to the touchline on a diagonal run and then headed for the by-line. Only belatedly did the Bridge back-four react to the danger; and when one of them moved out to challenge, Alex nimbly skipped past him and fired in a perfect cross for Foggy to head the ball home.

He should've done, too. But his aim was fractionally imperfect and when the ball thudded back into play off the inside of the upright the goalkeeper's flailing arm was able to divert it high over the bar. A second chance presented itself from the corner kick when Karl-Heinz dragged the ball down from a miscued defensive lunge and tried a left-foot shot into the corner. Once again, though, luck was with Bridge: another defender stuck out a foot and from his instep the ball ricocheted into the waiting arms of a grateful goalie. After that, Alex found he had

his own personal marker who proved impossible to shake off.

Something really special was needed to
unlock Bridge's defences and it came from
an unlikely quarter. For a long period Danny
Loxham had been inactive. With their concentration on defence, Friday Bridge weren't
mounting many attacks. So when the ball
reached him from a speculative long-range
lob, Danny kept possession. Dropping the
ball at his feet he took it upfield without
anyone considering challenging him until he
was over the half-way line. One or two
Rodale spectators anxiously recommended
that he get rid of it *now* and both Foggy and
Alex yelled for a pass.

Danny ignored them. Like many goal-
keepers he fancied his skills on the ball as an
outfield player and before joining the Kings
had been a capable winger with his school
team. The challenges he'd expected weren't
forthcoming, opponents continuing to retreat
in front of him in the belief he would pass
the ball to a team-mate. Danny did nothing
of the sort. Instead, he suddenly accelerated
and, seeing his opposite number well off his

line, let fly with his left foot.

It was a remarkably well struck shot – and it had power and direction – and it flew high over everyone's head until at last it dipped – and then it landed in the back of the net.

The ranks of Rodale supporters erupted. 'A goal in a thousand!' Clark Kelly reckoned.

'No, a goal in a million!' Serena Colmer corrected him. And no one disputed that claim. On the pitch, Friday Bridge players simply looked disbelieving, and no one could blame them. The Kings were literally dancing around one another in glee as they were ushered back to their own half by the ref for the restart.

Ricky, who'd been applauding as vigorously as anyone, grinned at Sam Saxton and held up both thumbs. 'Great stuff, great goal!' he chortled, hoping it might be seen as a peace-offering by the coach.

'Definitely!' Sam agreed. But he couldn't help adding a dagger-thrust: 'Took a defender to score it, though!' It also occurred to him that whatever else happened in this Final he'd have to give the man-of-the-match award to Danny if only for keeping the game alive when it looked perilously like defeat for the Kings.

Karl-Heinz was the player dominating Sam's thoughts. The stocky German wasn't playing at his best and yet he had still produced some examples of pure football skill, a hooked shot on the turn and a double-shuffle to evade a defender followed by a chip that just skimmed the bar. Any time he was near Friday Bridge's penalty area he might win the game for them. On the other hand, Sam's doubts about Karl-Heinz's stamina persisted. So should he bring him off, put on a fresh and eager runner?

'Boss, let me have a go,' demanded Davey Stroud, almost as if he'd been reading the coach's mind. 'I can do a lot of damage out there. Get a goal for sure.'

Sam shook his head. He didn't doubt that Davey would work until he dropped with exhaustion if necessary but he didn't have Karl-Heinz's talent to unfasten a defence playing with the composure of Bridge's. Moreover, if it came to a penalty shoot-out, as now seemed inevitable, he wanted the German to take one of the kicks. From the spot, he might be the deadliest shooter of them all.

As the final minutes ticked away mistakes crept in and one or two blunders were spectacular: a sliced miskick from Kieren that sent the ball ballooning over his own crossbar, a back-header at the other end by a Bridge defender that was only just clawed out of the net by his athletic goalkeeper, a silly, petulant squabble by two players for possession which ended with both flat on their backs on the pitch and getting reproving finger-shakes from the ref. The big pitch had taken its toll of the stamina of most of the players and the ball stayed out of the net for a final score of 1–1.

'Oh, this isn't fair, this is putting too much pressure on young players,' said Karen Rowley when she realized there was to be a shoot-out to find the winners. She remembered all too well Josh's agony when he missed with his kick the last time. Josh himself, only a spectator for this match, said nothing. He was still trying to forget what he regarded as the worst moment of his life.

'Oh, I don't know about that,' Serena

replied. 'Just look at the excitement on their faces. Two minutes ago they were exhausted, now they're definitely on a high.'

No one overhearing that comment risked mentioning what the boys' reaction would be if Friday Bridge won the coveted trophy.

While most of the spectators moved to get a better view of the end where the shoot-out would take place, the ref talked to the coaches and received their lists of names of players and the order in which the kicks would be taken; each side would take five and then, if the scores were still level, it would be down to sudden death. A coin was tossed up and the Bridge coach called correctly. 'Your lot can go first,' he told Sam, hoping to increase the pressure on the Kings that Karen Rowley spoke out about.

It rested now on the broad shoulders of Karl-Heinz Bruggemann, Sam's choice to shoot first because everyone knew how cool he was in almost any situation on the pitch. So far Karl-Heinz had, to Rodale's disappointment, contributed little to the match. That would not matter a jot if he put the ball in the net *now*. With his customary lack of expression, Karl-Heinz placed the ball on the spot, turned, took three paces, swung round and, with his right foot, swept the ball well wide of the goalkeeper into the right-hand side of the net.

As the Rodale supporters and other players roared their delight the Bridge keeper rushed to the ref, protesting he hadn't been ready for the kick. 'Well, you should've been,' the official told him unsympathetically. 'I blew the whistle.'

There was no doubt that this minor controversy unnerved the next kicker. He'd seen his team-mate's fury and his coach's flapping arms and expressions of disbelief and he knew that now, if possible, it was even more important that he, too, should score.

He hit it hard and his direction was quite good. But not good enough. For Danny waited until he saw which way the ball was going before flinging himself full-length to catch it almost on the line. Pandemonium! Horror on the faces of the Bridge players, huge sighs of relief among the Rodale contingent.

Danny, still on a high after his brilliant goal in open play and his save just now, was practically as quick as Karl-Heinz with his shot, which he crashed high into the net, just as he had done against Clocklane in the first round of the Cup. Then, waving to his jubilant fans, he returned to the goal-line to face Friday Bridge's second kicker. This time he didn't have to exert himself at all. The tall, uncoordinated-looking Bridge boy toe-ended the ball well wide of the upright, an embarrassingly awful shot.

'Two-nil up, we *must* win it now!' Foggy exulted, though most of his listeners wished he hadn't risked bringing bad luck down on them for expressing that kind of certainty. After all, some parents present couldn't even bear to look when the kicks were being taken.

Alex was next. Sam had deliberately held him back, knowing that Alex would be desperate to match any achievement by Karl-Heinz. Alex, of course, lacked nothing in confidence and his long run at the ball underlined his determination to whack the ball with all his power. Which he did. And it flew like a cannon shot beyond the goalkeeper's reach just inside the post. Alex leapt high with joy and Ricky and Sam led the applause.

Three-nil down, Friday Bridge simply had to score now or lose the game. There was hardly a sound as their left-winger, easily their most impressive player on the day, placed the ball on the spot, surveyed it from above as if speaking to it privately, and then took four precise backward steps. As the ball was struck Danny chose to go one way – and was easily beaten when it passed him on the other side. It was the brilliant goalkeeper's only mistake of the match. But it allowed Friday Bridge to dream once more of seizing the Cup.

Dominic, one of the favourites for the Goal Kings' player-of-the-season award, was to take what could be the clinching kick. It was he who scored the final goal in the previous shoot-out when he hit the ball close to the base of the upright. That was his target again as he took his time over placing the ball and subduing the flutterings in his stomach.

He knew, everyone present knew, that if he converted this kick the Cup was the Kings'. It was as simple, and horrifyingly difficult, as that. 'Do it for us, Dominic, just do it for us!' Sam Saxton was urging under his breath.

Jane Allenby watched without being able to think of anything at all; her eyes could see but her mind somehow was blank. Alex was biting his lip so hard it was white.

Dominic's aim wasn't as precise as it had been against Clocklane yet it was still good enough to defeat the keeper, who just managed to get his fingertips on the ball but couldn't keep it out of the net.

'YES!' roared Ricky and Sam simultaneously. 'We've done it. We've won the Cup!'

And the Rodale Goal Kings began celebrations that looked as though they might last for ever.

If you particularly enjoy reading about football, why not try some of these other Faber children's books?

Goal Kings by Michael Hardcastle

BOOK ONE: Shoot-Out
BOOK TWO: Eye for a Goal
BOOK THREE: And Davey Must Score
BOOK FOUR: They All Count

Life in the Junior Football League can be tough. This adventure-packed series follows the dramas and excitements – on and off the pitch – in the lives of Goal Kings JFC.

Own Goal by Michael Hardcastle

Russell is passionate about football but he has a problem: he scores own goals. Then, amazingly, he discovers a footballing talent he never dared dream of.

One Kick by Michael Hardcastle

Jamie finds that all is not fair play on the

field, and makes a mistake that is to haunt him for weeks and almost put a stop to his footballing career...

Second Chance by Michael Hardcastle

Scott is an ace striker. But when he moves to a school where soccer comes a poor second to cricket, he faces an unexpected and difficult challenge...

Frances Fairweather: Demon Striker!
by Derek Smith

Frances is so obsessed with football that she gets thrown out of the girls' team, and the boys' team won't have her either. Drastic measures are called for: Frances decides to become 'Frank'...

Faber children's books are available from bookshops. For a complete catalogue, please write to: The Children's Marketing Department, Faber and Faber, 3 Queen Square, London WC1N 3AU.